CONSPIRACY
in Corinth

To: Bailey Williams with best wishes!

by
Phil Hardwick

Phil Hardwick 12/3/99

QUAIL RIDGE PRESS
Brandon, Mississippi

On the cover: Alcorn County Courthouse
Photo by Gordon Denman

Illustrations by Phil Hardwick

Other books in Phil Hardwick's Mississippi Mysteries Series:

Found in Flora
Justice in Jackson
Captured in Canton
Newcomer in New Albany
Vengeance in Vicksburg
Collision in Columbia

To be included on the Mississippi Mysteries mailing list, please send your name and complete mailing address to:

QUAIL RIDGE PRESS
P. O. Box 123 • Brandon, MS 39043
1-800-343-1583

DEDICATION

This book is dedicated to those who
have paid the ultimate sacrifice
on the field of battle,
especially the 1,738 soldiers
who died in the Battle of Corinth
on October 4th and 5th, 1862.

ACKNOWLEDGMENTS

Dear Reader:

They say that 7 is a lucky number. If that is so, then I feel that I have found a bit of luck in writing number 7 in the Mississippi Mysteries Series. I'm lucky because I was able to spend time in Corinth.

While doing research for this book, I spent several days in Corinth talking to several interesting and wonderful people. They deserve mention here.

First, thanks to Emily Stokes and Norman Isbell, Executive Director and President of Main Street Corinth. It is Main Street Corinth and its Board of Directors who took on this project and have supported it from the beginning. They are to be commended. One only has to walk around downtown Corinth to see the fruits of their labor.

Many others in Corinth were helpful to me in learning about their community. Charlotte and Luke Doehner, proprietors of the Generals' Quarters, made me feel like part of the family. The entire crew at Borroum's Drug Store spent much time telling me about the history of the store and their family. It is a Mississippi treasure that everyone should visit. And you can order a Slugburger at the soda fountain. Kristy White and Margaret Rogers at the Corinth Museum gave me part of their valuable time and provided valuable information about Roscoe Turner, one of the state's most colorful figures. A special thanks to Frank Simmons, Jr. for his contribution on the history of the Pickwick Theater.

In Jackson, there are those who deserve mention. Dr. Will Sorey was generous with his time and counsel on some of the medical matters in the book. My wife and children are also to be thanked for giving me the time to work on my pet project. Last, but certainly not least, is the staff at Quail Ridge Press, especially Cyndi, who does her best to keep me on schedule, and Gwen, who serves as editor-in-chief. It is gratifying to see a publisher in today's competitive book business that cares about doing something for the community instead of only making a big profit.

I hope you enjoy *Conspiracy In Corinth* and that you will take the time to visit the Gateway City. If you already live in Corinth, I urge you to get a copy of the self-guided tour and learn about the uniqueness of your community. Many of us don't know what is in our own backyard.

Sincerely,

Phil Hardwick

Chapter 1

"This is Pace McHatten in Corinth, Mississippi, calling for Jack Boulder," said the deep voice on the answering machine on the end table beside the living room sofa. "Please call me regarding an urgent matter. It's not what you think it is, Jack."

Andrew Jackson Boulder, private investigator in Jackson, Mississippi, replayed the message. Then he played it a third time. Then the memories started rising as if a water pipe had burst, filling his living room and his brain with scenes buried a long time ago. Cloudy images from a war in the late '60s in a land far away. Murky images of explosions and gunfire and dirty, putrid rice paddies. Vivid images of a fellow soldier who grasped Boulder's fatigues and whose last, panicky words were, "Don't let me die, Jack." Boulder told his friend not to worry, that he could count on Jack. After all, it was the last month of their tour of duty. Minutes later, the Medivac Huey landed only 30 yards away, its rotor blades announcing its arrival with a "pop-pop-pop" sound. Boulder slung his dying buddy over his shoulder like a sack of potatoes, sloshed through the muck, and dumped him inside the pulsating helicopter. Boulder knew that his comrade in arms was dead the instant he set him down because his head hit the floor first. He had let down his buddy, Pace McHatten, Jr.

They had met in Military Police School in Ft.

Gordon, Georgia. They were the only two recruits from Mississippi, and because of that fact had become instant buddies. Boulder told his new pal how his parents were shocked when he had enlisted, but they eventually supported his decision. McHatten shared the fact that his parents felt betrayed when he joined. McHatten, Jr. was supposed to go to Ole Miss undergraduate and law school, then return to practice law in Corinth with his father. McHatten's father was a prominent attorney, and the father let his son know plainly that he did not approve of his son's joining the Army, especially as an enlisted man. If a McHatten had to be in the military, it should be as an officer.

The Mississippi boys were separated after graduation. Boulder was sent to the Presidio in San Francisco and McHatten to Ft. Sam Houston in San Antonio, Texas. They stayed in touch and even visited each other once. Boulder showed McHatten the San Francisco night life and McHatten returned the favor in San Antonio. As luck would have it, both were later assigned to the same unit in Vietnam for their last 18 months of military service. They spent many nights talking about going back to the United States and joining a police department together. McHatten argued for their joining the Bexar County Sheriff's Department in San Antonio, while Boulder held out for the San Francisco P.D.. Eventually, they compromised and decided that the Mississippi Highway Safety Patrol could not do without their services. It did not turn out as planned. McHatten returned to Corinth in a flag-draped coffin. Boulder joined the St. Louis, Missouri Police Department.

The funeral was the hardest part. Boulder fought with himself many sleepless nights about whether he really wanted to go. In the end, he decided it would be the best thing. He would tell McHatten's parents what a good soldier their son had been, and how he had died valiantly. It would be a difficult thing to do, but they deserved as much. At the visitation in the funeral home he approached the McHattens, prepared to make his speech. When he introduced himself, Mr. McHatten turned on him like a pit bull, demanding to know who he thought he was coming to the funeral of someone whom he had let die in battle. McHatten, Sr. came at Boulder in a rage, backing him up against a wall in a shower of spittle and a whispered yell that could not be absorbed by the velvet drapes of the funeral parlor. Boulder stood at attention, his back literally to the wall, as McHatten, Sr. continued his muffled tirade. Finally, Mrs. McHatten came to the rescue, and Boulder left the funeral home and Corinth.

He never heard from the McHattens again. Until today. What was it? Twenty-five years now. Boulder had spent 20 years on the St. Louis Police Department, retiring three years ago as a homicide detective. A week after his retirement party he moved back to his boyhood home of Jackson and opened shop as a private investigator. Life had treated him well. He had a good business doing what he liked. He had renewed a relationship with his high school sweetheart, who was now a powerful Jackson corporate attorney. He lived in a nice condominium overlooking Smith Park in downtown of the Capital City. He even went middle-aged crazy and bought a 1968 Chevrolet Camaro, the model of his first car, and fully restored it. And he had stored all those memories of America's most pathetic war in the back of a mental closet somewhere. But the pipe had burst. He held out his right hand in front of him. It was shaking.

Boulder played the message one more time. "It's not what you think it is." The words had no meaning to Jack. What was McHatten saying? Boulder knew that the only way to stop from drowning in the mental morass was to make a decision. Right now. No beating around the bush. And so he did. He decided that the past was past, and he was not going to go there again.

Making that decision was like opening a floodgate and letting the water of his memory run out on the street. Boulder felt good about himself again. He looked down at his hand. Not shaking this time. Maybe the past was letting go of him for good.

Suddenly the telephone sounded its electronic warble. Boulder jumped, then picked up the receiver out of habit. "Jack Boulder," he said officially.

"Jack, this is Pace McHatten. Don't hang up."

"What do you want?" The words were soft and cautious. It didn't come out as "What do YOU want?"

"I have a problem which requires the services of a private investigator and I was told that you are one of the best in Mississippi. I'm representing a man who is about to be charged with murder. I really need your help. Could we at least talk about it face-to-face?"

"I thought you had said all you had to say to me a long time ago," said Boulder.

"Look," said McHatten firmly. "I'm not calling you for anything other than official business. I have a client who needs all the resources I can bring to his case. When you hear the facts, I think you will agree. Frankly, it's my client who needs you. I'll pay you $2,000 just to come up here and listen to the facts."

"When do you want me there?"

"Tomorrow morning."

"I'll call you back."

"When?" asked McHatten.

"After I see if I can clear my calendar. It's 8:30 now. I'll call you back within an hour."

"I'll be waiting."

Boulder hung up the telephone, walked over to the French doors that led out onto his balcony overlooking Smith Park. He leaned against a black, wrought iron rail. It was the middle of summer and the trees were full and green. As usual, the humidity was high. He enjoyed living here in a two-story condominium that he owned outright. It was also his place of business, the third bedroom being his office. It was filled with state-of-the-art photography equipment, computer, fax and other supplies that private investigators used from time to time. No secretary was needed.

The telephone rang again. He picked it up on the third ring.

"You're out early this morning," chirped Laura Webster. "I could see you from my office."

Boulder took the cordless phone, walked back onto the balcony and waved at the black-glassed, upper floors of the Deposit Guaranty Plaza Building where her law firm was located.

"I was just about to call you," he said.

"Sure you were," she said with a teasing tone.

"Ever heard of a lawyer in Corinth named Pace McHatten?"

"Of course," she replied. "He was president of the State Bar a few years ago, and he's been a judge—a chancellor, I think. Old line. Respected." There was a pause. "Why do you ask?"

"He called today and asked if I could help him with a case."

"You should feel honored."

"I never told you about Pace McHatten, Jr., did I?"

"Is this a war story?" she asked.

"I'm afraid so."

"Let's save it for tonight," she said. "You're still my

date for the Symphony Ball next week, aren't you?"

"You know it."

They hung up and Boulder squatted down on the floor and did 50 pushups without working up a sweat. He did this every day just to keep his upper body toned. He also ran at least two miles every day to keep his weight in the 180-pound range, the same place it was when he graduated from the St. Louis Police Academy almost 25 years ago. He figured that pushups also helped him think. When he finished he went back to the telephone and dialed Pace McHatten's number.

"I'll be in your office at 1:00 tomorrow afternoon," he told the lawyer.

Chapter 2

On Tuesday morning at 8:00 a.m. Jack Boulder turned his Camaro from Interstate 55 onto the north-bound lane of the Natchez Trace Parkway and began the 218-mile trip to Corinth. The previous night he had cal-culated that it would take at least four hours to make the drive. The most direct route was "the Trace," although it probably was not the fastest, owing to the fact that it had a strictly enforced 50 mile per hour speed limit. The U.S. Park Rangers had a well-deserved reputation for ticketing speeders on the tree-laced ribbon of asphalt that ran from Nashville to Natchez. On the other hand, the shade of the trees made it a degree or two cooler, an important fact to one who is driving a car without air conditioning. Boulder relaxed as the 327-cubic-inch V-8 engine powered the car of his passion through the tall pines.

Last night had been good. He had told Laura all about Pace McHatten, Jr. and how the soldier from Corinth had died in his arms in Vietnam. He also told her about the funeral incident. She listened as only a caring woman can. Her advice was certain and unam-biguous. He should go to Corinth. He didn't tell her that he already told McHatten he was coming.

At 11:30 a.m. Boulder exited the Trace at Tupelo, and headed north on U.S. Highway 45. Soon he encountered a "Welcome to Corinth" sign printed on a large base supporting two white columns that were no doubt Corinthian.

Corinth is a town steeped in history, especially Civil War history. Known as Mississippi's Gateway City, Corinth lies in the northeast corner of the Magnolia State, 89 miles from Memphis and 168 miles from Birmingham, Alabama. Location is important to any city, but to Corinth it has been especially significant. In 1861, Corinth was the crossroads of two strategic railroads: Memphis to Charleston and Mobile to Ohio. During the Civil War, Union and Confederate armies occupied the city at one time or another. The little town of 1,200 residents saw over 300,000 troops stationed in and around Corinth during the war years. At least 200 top Confederate or Federal generals were stationed in Corinth, and over 100 skirmishes and/or raids occurred in the area.

On October 4th and 5th, 1862, the Battle of Corinth was fought, resulting in Federal losses of 315, with 1,812 wounded, and 232 captured or missing. The Confederates had losses of 1,423, with 5,692 wounded and 2,268 captured or missing. The Battle of Corinth was one of the fiercest and bloodiest of the war. Analysts consider it the beginning of the end of the War in the West.

Today, visitors and tourists are offered, among other things, a 23-stop self-guided tour directed by a fold-out brochure from the Corinth Area Tourism Promotion

Council. Stops include battlefields, significant buildings, cemeteries, and historic sites. For Civil War buffs, it is considered a must.

The law office of Pace McHatten was in the middle of the block on Waldron Street, directly across from the south side of the Alcorn County Courthouse. It was a two-story building of dark red brick, with a large glass window on the first floor façade and three tall double-hung windows in the second floor. McHatten was a man who believed that every lawyer's office should be in the shade of, if not the sight of, the local courthouse. Also in sight of McHatten's office was a statue of Colonel William P. Rogers of the Second Texas unit, a Confederate officer killed in the Battle of Corinth.

Boulder parked his Camaro in a pull-up parking place at the front door. As he entered the office, he was greeted by a receptionist who looked like she could have been the homecoming queen at Corinth High School five years earlier. She was planted behind a wraparound secretary's desk that fitted against a credenza against the side wall of the office. A large computer monitor and keyboard were positioned on the desk so that a visitor saw only the maze of wiring on the back of the computer equipment. Her desktop had one small stack of legal-sized papers, but was otherwise uncluttered. He noticed on the credenza a five-by-seven, gold-framed color photo of her, a man of similar age and a small child. The office had hardwood floors throughout and exposed brick walls. Boulder thought the air-conditioning was set too low because he was already cold. He introduced himself.

"Yes, I'm Amy," she replied with a pleasant smile. "I'll tell Judge McHatten that you are here." She reached down, picked up the telephone receiver, pushed a button and said, "Mr. Boulder here to see you, sir." She replaced the receiver and turned to Boulder. "Just go right up those stairs."

Boulder thanked her and ascended the stairs to the second floor. At the top was a small landing and closed door. He opened it and walked into a huge office that must have been 20 feet by 80 feet. A large desk was positioned at one end of the room, with its back to the front windows. In front of the desk was a sitting area, complete with coffee table, oriental rug, six captain's chairs and a sofa that faced the desk. At the other end of the office was a large conference table that could easily seat 14. End tables, floor lamps and other office accessories were strategically placed. Bookcases lined the side walls at the desk end of the room, while framed certificates, licenses and a few small paintings decorated the conference table end. On the far wall behind the conference table was a wall-to-wall, floor-to-ceiling cabinet made of dark wood. The United States and Mississippi flags were positioned on the appropriate sides. Boulder wondered cynically if he should salute.

As Boulder entered the room, McHatten rose from

behind the desk, but remained standing in place. He was a tall man, towering six feet, four inches from the floor. He wore thick black glasses, and had thick white hair and a matching mustache. If he had a goatee, the resemblance to Colonel Sanders would be striking. He wore a vested blue and white seersucker suit. His arms remained down by his side.

"Thank you for coming, Boulder," growled the attorney. "I called the chief investigator with the Highway Patrol and told him I needed the best private investigator south of Highway 82 for a very important case. He called the chief of detectives with the Jackson Police Department and was informed that you are the best. I need someone from out of town who can be objective. It's difficult to find someone in Corinth who doesn't know, or isn't related to, someone else in north Mississippi, if you know what I mean?"

"I'm honored."

"You should be," said McHatten. He sat down in a high-backed judge's chair behind the desk. Boulder grasped the top of a chair facing the coffee table, spun it around on one leg so that he faced the judge, and took a seat. "What I've got here is a client who stands to be convicted of murdering his wife if I don't either settle the case or prove he didn't do it. I don't like settling cases. The accused either did it or didn't do it. Settling is not only like kissing your sister, it's a mutation of justice."

"Did your client do it?"

"Frankly, I don't know. The evidence is rather compelling. But the evidence doesn't fit the man." He reached down, picked up a file folder and opened it. "Let me give you the facts as they are now known by the district attorney. Four weeks ago—Friday, June 18—in the middle of the day, an ambulance was summoned to the home of Dr. and Mrs. Marlin Haines. When the ambulance arrived, Mrs. Haines was found collapsed in the kitchen. She had no pulse and resuscitation efforts failed. The police were summoned and arrived almost immediately. She was taken to the medical center, where she was pronounced dead on arrival. An autopsy was performed the following day. The cause of death was listed as inconclusive pending further analysis by the crime lab. Last Friday the tests came back from the lab. It showed that she had enough acetaminophen in her to kill a horse. One of my sources in the District Attorney's Office says that they intend to indict him for murder unless some new evidence turns up."

"Who called for the ambulance?" asked Boulder.

"Marlin—rather, Dr. Haines—did."

"What about his relationship with Mrs. Haines? Any marital problems?"

"That's where the tide turns against Dr. Haines. He is 65; she was under 40. They had been married for nine months. In that time, Dr. Haines turned from being the most cordial, outgoing man in Corinth to practically becoming a recluse. He had an active practice and worked at least eight hours every day. Two months after they were married he announced that he had decided to start closing at noon every day. Not only that, he quietly resigned from every civic and community project he was involved in. He quit as president of the Corinth Museum board in the middle of his term and resigned as a board member of the Corinth Downtown Association. He even quit teaching his Sunday School class at the First Baptist Church. He had been teaching that class for 30 years. He quit going places and getting out. You would have had to have known him, but his personality changed. All he did was go to his office at eight each morning, see a few patients and go back home at noon."

"What kind of doctor was he?" asked Boulder, sitting back in the chair.

"Last of the breed, I guess," replied McHatten. "He was the classic general practitioner. I think he was an internist. He didn't do surgery. Just diagnosed and prescribed medicine. But the thing about him was that he could tell what was wrong with somebody when others couldn't. He had a gift for that."

"How did he meet his wife?"

"Good question," said McHatten, leaning back in his big chair. "He went to Florida to some medical convention about a year ago. He came back to Corinth acting like a high school boy who had found his first love. Then he would be gone every weekend. Suddenly, he returns with her and announces that they are man and wife. I've never seen him happier."

"Was she his first wife?"

"His third," said the lawyer flatly as if anticipating the question.

"And his first two?"

"His first wife was killed in an automobile accident on their honeymoon. He survived with minor injuries. Two years later he married Rosemary. They were married for . . ." He paused and looked at the ceiling. "It must have been 40 years. One son. A doctor in Houston."

"Is the son coming back?"

"For what?"

"If my father were charged with murder, I think I would want to be with him," said Boulder.

"His son is a very important cancer specialist at a world-renowned medical center," said McHatten, becoming agitated. A snideness crept into his tone of voice and he leaned forward slightly. He narrowed his bushy eyebrows and aimed a stare at Boulder like a rifle to a target. "At least he has a son who could come home if he really needed to."

Boulder didn't move, but his face began turning blood red. He arose slowly, leaning toward the lawyer like a mountain lion about to leap on its prey. He looked down at McHatten and took a slow, deep breath. "I'll be going now," the private investigator said firmly. "I've heard all I need to hear about this case. And you can keep your filthy $2,000."

He turned and walked out the door, leaving McHatten speechless at his desk.

Chapter 3

Boulder marched out to his car, started the engine with a loud rev, and jammed the transmission into reverse gear. He backed out onto the street, then reached down and shoved the transmission lever into first. He mashed the accelerator, let out on the clutch and almost burned rubber as the car began to leap forward. Suddenly, in front of him, less than three feet from his front bumper, stood Pace McHatten, hands by his side like a gunfighter about to draw. Boulder slammed on the brakes just before hitting him. McHatten remained standing at his position, like the statue of the Confederate soldier across the street. Boulder looked around the courthouse square as if pleading for help from any source. McHatten took a step forward, walked to the driver's side window, looming over Boulder.

"I hope you will forgive me," he said. "I was out of line. Please come back inside."

"No thanks. I don't need this, nor do I deserve this."

"You're right," said McHatten. "You're absolutely right. I know how you must feel about me. Please. Dr. Haines needs your help. He's not only my client, he's my friend. What do you say?"

Boulder lowered his head and stared down at his speedometer. His eyes lost focus as a mixture of feelings came over him. He knew he should leave, but there was something pulling at him to stay. He didn't like unfinished business. There was another thing. When he looked at McHatten he saw more than a gruff, old, egotistical, self-centered man. He saw the memory of the friend who had died in his arms. Maybe it was in his eyes, maybe in his mannerisms. But it was there. Make no mistake about it. Boulder took a slow, deep breath and looked up at McHatten.

"I believe you owe me $2,000," said Boulder.

"Yes," replied McHatten with renewed enthusiasm. "Come on back inside and I'll make out a check."

Boulder parked the car, and they went back inside to the upstairs office. They sat down again in the same chairs. McHatten reached down and removed a large, black leather checkbook from his lower right hand desk drawer. He began writing out a check. There was a tearing sound as McHatten withdrew the check. "This should make your trip worthwhile," he said, handing Boulder a check for $2,000.

Boulder folded it without looking at it and deposited it in his pocket. "How did his second wife die?"

McHatten smiled slightly and leaned back in his chair. "She had a heart attack."

"Was there an autopsy?" asked Boulder.

"No. There was no reason to believe there was foul play. She simply died in her sleep. Would that we will all be so lucky."

"When did she die?" asked Boulder.

The attorney raised his hand to his jaw and said, "Let's see. It would be about a year ago. Yes. It was the weekend of the Fourth of July."

"How long have you known Dr. Haines?"

"All my life. We grew up together."

"Were you—rather, are you—social friends?"

"You might say that," said McHatten. "It's a small town."

"When can I talk to your client?"

"Right now, if you would like. He's at home." The lawyer picked up a telephone and barked, "Get Doc Haines on the line." He held it to his ear for a moment, then said into the mouthpiece. "Doc, I'm sending that private investigator over to see you. Tell him anything he wants to know, you hear?" After saying goodbye he turned to Boulder. "Doc lives right up the street on Fillmore." He reached down for a pen and paper and wrote something. "Here's the address. You can't miss it. Come back when you finish."

Boulder took the paper and went outside to his car. He drove around the courthouse, then up Fillmore Street to the address. It was a two-story red brick house, with a small stoop instead of a large front porch like most of the other houses in the block. The yard was scattered with tall trees, and azalea bushes hugged a white fence. Right out of one of those magazines that feature homes in the South. Boulder pushed a round, white button at the door and heard chimes from inside. The brass knob made a clanking sound as the door opened. An older man in his late '60s opened the door. He was stooped slightly and slow moving. Boulder knew the look. He had seen it before when a family member or friend had been killed. It was the look of numbness, of shock. The kind of look that indicated that the mind was far away. The man had gray hair, a dirty kind of gray instead of the distinguished variety. His nose was red and larger than average. He wore navy dress slacks, a white dress shirt, dark blue suspenders and a pair of house slippers. There were no socks. The ankles were lily-white. There was a day's worth of salt and pepper gray stubble on his face.

"Please, come in," the man said in a kind voice. "I'm Marlin Haines." He waved Boulder toward the inside. As Boulder passed by him he detected the odor of alcohol. "Can I get you some coffee?"

"That would be fine," said Boulder in spite of the fact that he had no desire for coffee on this hot Mississippi afternoon. It gave him time to absorb the living room of Marlin Haines, M.D. He sat down on a yellow sofa and scanned the environment as Dr. Haines headed slowly for the kitchen. There was nothing unusual about the setting, except for one thing—there was nothing personal about it. The paintings on the wall were of horses or landscapes and the furniture looked like it belonged in a fine home. Four windows, two facing the front and two facing the side, gave the room plenty of natural light. Boulder decided that he might as well be in the showroom of an Ethan Allen furniture store. No clues to the man here. He got up and walked through a short hallway toward the back of the house. He heard the tinkling of cups and headed in that direction. He emerged into a large kitchen and breakfast nook. Doc Haines had his back to him as he poured black liquid from a coffee maker on the counter.

"I take it black," said Boulder.

"Good," said the doctor, turning with a blue mug in his right hand. His hand shook slightly and a few drops spilled on the floor. Acting as though he didn't see it, he handed the mug to Boulder and said, "If you like strong coffee, this should be just what you need."

Boulder accepted the dark liquid and sat down at the table against the wall.

"Mind if I ask you a few questions, Doc?"

"No. Go ahead." He sat down at the table. "Mac said that's what you needed to do."

"Where was your wife when you found her?"

"Right there," he said, pointing to a spot in the middle of the floor.

"Did she have a pulse?"

"None at all," he replied.

"What was she wearing?"

"Let's see," he said, scratching the back of his head and narrowing his eyes. "I'm not really sure."

"A dress or slacks and blouse?" asked Boulder

"It was slacks and blouse. The blouse was white, I believe."

"Describe the day up to that point," instructed Boulder.

"I woke up at 5:30 a.m., as usual," said physician. "I had a bowl of cereal. Raisin Bran, I think it was. It's important to get plenty of fiber in your diet. It could have been All Bran. Would you like for me to check the cabinet?" he asked, leaning toward the other side of the room.

"No. That's not necessary."

"I guess that's kind of stupid, isn't it? Who cares what kind of cereal I had? But diet is important to good health. People should realize that." He paused and expelled a small laugh, then shook his head from side to side as if to say, "Tsk, tsk."

"Go ahead with what you did after breakfast," instructed Boulder.

"Then I went to the office until noon. I can get you my patient list if you need it. Only thing unusual was the Ludlow boy. He got stung by a brown recluse spider the week before. Didn't tell anybody. Now his skin is eating away from it. But he'll be alright."

"Did you call home before you left your office?"

"No," said the doctor. "I just came on home. I found Melanie collapsed right there on the floor. I called 911 and the ambulance came quickly, but it was too late."

"Why did you call for an ambulance if she didn't

have a pulse?"

"I don't know. It just seemed the natural thing to do."

"The autopsy determined that she had a lot of acetaminophen in her body," said Boulder. "Can you explain that?"

"Mr. Boulder, my wife was in a great deal of pain. It was necessary for her to get relief."

"What kind of pain?"

"Migraine headaches," said Dr. Haines. "She had a severe case."

"Did you know that when you married her?"

"No," said the doctor. "But it wouldn't have made any difference. She made me feel like a man again. I hadn't felt the way she made me feel in a long time."

"How did you meet her?"

"At a medical convention in Miami. She worked for the hotel. In the marketing department. After the convention was over, I went back to Miami to see her several times. One thing led to another. I knew there would be talk in town when we came back, but she was something else."

"Doc," said Boulder, adding a long pause for effect. "What do YOU think happened to your wife?"

Dr. Marlin Haines put his hands together, lacing the fingers, and placed them in his lap. "I wonder if she might have committed suicide," he said with a sigh.

Boulder let the words settle. He took a sip of coffee.

He knew that he didn't have to ask any more questions. The doctor was ready to talk. The detective had seen it many times. Once the right questions were asked, the right gestures were made, and the feeling of trust established, a person would pour out his guts. Boulder had gotten many confessions in his days as a police officer by just listening to what others had to say. He knew instinctively that a person has a strong emotional need to be understood. Was the doctor about to confess?

"I told her she was taking too much pain medicine," said Dr. Haines slowly, his head dropping. "She wouldn't listen to me. I told her that she needed treatment. She began to get depressed and irritable. She stopped eating properly. Wouldn't go outside the house. I thought she was beginning to have second thoughts about marrying me. Did you know that she was only 35? The town certainly must have had a lot of fun at my expense. The old coot who goes off and gets a trophy wife." He sighed, then continued. "It wasn't like that. We really had something. She just got sick."

"So how did she commit suicide?" asked Boulder. "You can't O.D. on non-aspirin pain reliever."

"Oh, but you can," said Doctor Haines, raising his right hand to make the point. "Acetaminophen can be toxic when taken in large doses. Ten grams in an adult can be fatal. Especially when someone has been taking it daily in large doses. The liver just can't take it. I had been telling her to reduce her dosage. She just went to the store and bought more. In stronger doses, no less." His lower lip began to quiver. His voice broke. "I should have seen it coming."

Boulder sat there for a few more minutes, slowing sipping his now lukewarm coffee. Whether Dr. Haines was telling the truth or not was something Boulder did not evaluate. He knew that he must remain objective. Nevertheless, he felt sorry for this man.

Chapter 4

Boulder went back to McHatten's office and briefed the attorney on his interview with the doctor. The lawyer listened intently, then said, "Good. Damn good. There's enough doubt there. A jury has got to have proof beyond a reasonable doubt. We're in good shape if we go to trial. But I don't want to go to trial."

"So what do you want me to do?" asked Boulder.

"What if this were St. Louis or wherever you worked, and you were the detective in charge of this case? How would you handle it? What would you do?"

"Assuming that we believed this was a homicide," replied Boulder. "I would interview everyone who knew the doctor well, including his family. I would reconstruct the last 48 hours of the deceased's life. Just like it was a plane crash. I'd talk to everybody she talked to; I'd find out where she went and even what she had for breakfast."

"Sounds good," said McHatten. "Do it."

"But . . ."

"No buts. A thousand a day. Plus expenses."

Before Boulder could say anything else, McHatten picked up the telephone and got his secretary on the line. "Marilyn, get Mr. Boulder a reservation at the Generals' Quarters beginning tonight. He'll be staying in Corinth a few days. Tell them to direct-bill the law firm." He hung up the phone and pasted a sly smile on his face. "I need your help, Boulder. Don't let me down."

Boulder thought about telling him where he could stick that telephone, but then he thought better of it. A thousand a day had gotten his attention.

"It's getting late in the day," the attorney said. "Get on over to the Generals' Quarters. You'll like it there. Get to work and call me when you have something to report."

"First, I need the names of Dr. Haines' family members, office staff and close friends."

They spent the next few minutes putting together a list. McHatten referred to the local telephone directory for numbers. "These will get you started. He has three sisters here in town. The names of his employees are also there. You can go now."

Boulder stood up, turned and left. No handshake. No goodbye. McHatten was a hard man. Someone who had ice water in his veins. It was easy to see why his son had chosen to escape.

The Generals' Quarters is located at 924 Fillmore Street, at the corner of Fillmore and Linden, only three blocks north of the heart of downtown and only a few houses from that of Dr. Haines. The area is residential, featuring large homes on medium-sized lots with fences, tall trees and landscaping that always has something in bloom. From March to October the aroma of one flower or another fills the air. Boulder walked up

several steps into a glass-enclosed foyer that put him face-to-face with the front door. Before he could ring the bell he heard footsteps inside, then the opening of the door.

"You must be Mr. Boulder," said the attractive middle-aged woman standing in front of him. She had dark hair, fair skin and wore pink slacks and a white blouse. Behind her ear was a yellow No. 2 pencil. "Please come in. I'm Ann Beckwith. My husband and I own your home away from home." Boulder thanked her and she said, "You'll be in room number one. It's at the top of the stairs."

She led him up an open stairway to the second floor landing, where a sitting area with books and magazines that ranged from Civil War history to *People* magazine were laid out at the end of the hallway. Against the wall beside the door to room number one was a four-foot-high rack of movie videocassettes. She opened the door and led him inside to a high-ceilinged, but small room that had a natural gas fireplace and mantel against an outside wall. In the front corner was a 20-inch television with videocassette player built in. Against a back wall was a writing table on which rested a brass lamp and telephone. Three large windows facing the street gave the room an open feeling.

"This is a bed and breakfast, but tonight we would like to invite you to have supper with us, if you have no other plans," she said as she handed him a room key. "We'll look forward to seeing you downstairs at 6:00."

"I'll be there," he said as he closed the door. He went to the phone and called Laura, needing moral support as well as legal guidance from his girlfriend back in Jackson. She was still in her office and answered on the first ring of her direct line.

"So how is Corinth?" she asked with a smile that could only be heard and not seen.

"It's hard to tell," he said. "I've never seen so many four-way stop signs. They are at every intersection downtown. And other drivers wave you through, unlike Jackson where you get cut off."

"What did McHatten have to say?"

"He wants to get his client off. I don't think he really cares what happened to the deceased. He's not an easy man to get along with."

They chatted a few more minutes. Boulder remarked that Corinth looked like a modern-day Mayberry from what he could tell so far. They promised to keep in touch daily.

Boulder took out the list that McHatten had given him and began making telephone calls. In ten minutes he had made appointments to meet all three sisters the following day. Sylvia and Sadie would be at a certain downtown café at 8:30 a.m. and Sally would meet him at a restaurant at a golf course at noon. None of them seemed surprised to receive his telephone call.

There was a knock on his door. He opened it to see Ann Beckwith, the proprietor. She had a wide smile on her face. "Dinner is served."

She led him downstairs to a dining room off the main living room where a man was seated at the head of the table. He was also middle-aged, but was just the opposite of her. His hair was blonde and his skin had an olive, tanned look. The man was wearing a casual shirt with green and gold stripes, so Boulder felt right at home in his polo shirt and chinos. The table was set like a fancy restaurant, with several different-sized plates and more than one fork.

"Mr. Boulder, this is my husband. His name is also Jack."

"Pleased to meet you."

"Glad you could join us," said the man in an accent

that Boulder guessed as the Jersey suburbs of New York City. "I hope you don't mind lasagna," he said, standing up.

"Of course not. I love lasagna."

The other Jack disappeared through a swinging door as Ann followed. She returned momentarily with a pitcher of water and poured the glasses full. Then Jack reappeared with three salads. He had the moves of someone who had done this act many times. The two sat back down and Jack The Host raised his glass and said, "To our special guest. May he have much luck in Corinth."

"Do you know why I'm here?" asked Boulder, getting right to the point.

"We understand that Judge McHatten has hired you for a special case," said Ann.

"Did he tell you which case?"

"No," said Jack. "But it's not too hard to figure out that you are working on the Dr. Haines matter."

"You would be correct," said Boulder. "Did you know him?"

"Not really," he replied. "We're not originally from around this area. We're from up North."

Boulder took a bite of salad, then said, "Tell me about this house. It's beautiful."

Ann and her husband looked at each other and smiled as if flipping some kind of imaginary coin to see who would tell the story. Ann won.

"I'll tell you what I have been able to piece together. Keep in mind that all of what I say is not documented, but is believed to be accurate." Boulder nodded agreement and took a sip of wine as she continued. "The lot was given to Christ Episcopal Church in 1859. The rector at that time was Henry Drummond. A church and rectory were built on the site. Just before the Battle of Corinth in 1862, Father Drummond made a trip to Hattiesburg. He returned shortly after the battle by railroad and was shocked to see so many dead and wounded being laid out side-by-side at the rail station. He stayed at the rail station attending the wounded and helping as best as he could. When he finally returned to the church he discovered that only two rooms remained—the rest of the building was destroyed. Kate Cummins, a Confederate nurse, along with Drummond and other parishioners, began to rebuild, but the bank foreclosed when the first payment was not received. The sheriff's wife somehow got the property and she sold it to the Bynum brothers. The building became a house and was decorated by John and Fannie Dilworth Bynum. By the way, her father was the Treasurer of the Confederacy and the Treasurer of the State of Mississippi."

"There were no other owners until the late 1920s when Mr. and Mrs. John Ramer purchased the house. He owned Saville-Dubale Coffee Company, which merged with another company and then became

38

Maxwell House—that's why we serve Maxwell House coffee. During the Ramers' ownership it was operated as a tourist house. He died in 1946 and she continued operating it as 'Mrs. Ramer's Boarding House' until 1963. As many as 30 people lived here. There was a series of owners after that until we bought it."

"It's a fabulous place," said Boulder.

A lovely meal and good conversation followed. Finally Boulder said that he needed to get some sleep.

"I have a busy day tomorrow."

Chapter 5

District Attorney William Magowan strode into the conference room of his Corinth branch office and tossed a large, brown, legal-sized file jacket on the table. It landed with a splat, signaling to the three other attorneys that the weekly meeting of those responsible for prosecuting criminal cases in Alcorn and several other counties in northeast Mississippi had come to order.

"Let's go ahead and get right to the Haines case," he said impatiently. "I've only got 30 minutes."

Normally, Magowan was a man who had plenty of time. Or so it seemed. He had the uncanny gift of being a good listener. He was also thorough and decisive, knowing that no detail was too small in criminal cases. Well-known and admired in northeast Mississippi, he was an elected official who genuinely cared about the people. The voters cared about him, too. Now in his third term as district attorney, his popularity had grown steadily since his second year in office when he took on a well-organized gang that specialized in interstate transportation and distribution of stolen property. The gang allegedly had ties to an organized crime syndicate in Chicago and had been pursued for years with limited success by two agencies of the federal government. In the end, a local district attorney named William Magowan had courageously defeated a national crime cartel and sent its leader to prison. The case was featured on a cable television national crime show, and *Newsweek* magazine had done a profile on the local D.A. who did what the feds couldn't. Not since the days of Buford Pusser in neighboring McNairy County, Tennessee had a local legend grown as much as that of William Magowan.

He didn't exactly look a crime buster in the manner of Elliot Ness. With his stocky build, short height and full head of red hair, he could have been cast in the gangster roles usually played by James Cagney. Married, with two small kids, he was the toast of the town.

His crime-fighting efforts had attracted the attention of the state's political power brokers and he had been convinced to run for attorney general. Now in the middle of a party primary, he had turned into a harried man maintaining a district attorney job and running a statewide political race. His opponent, a trial lawyer from the Mississippi Gulf Coast, was daily calling for him to resign, claiming that criminals were walking the streets because the D.A. didn't have time to do his job. But nobody was listening to his opponent. The political columnists had already pronounced that it was Magowan's race to lose. His advisors told him to keep on doing what he was doing. Stay away from the controversial cases. Let the assistants handle the dynamite. Just be certain to attend every sweet potato, watermelon and tomato festival during the summer and leave the rest to the experienced politicos.

The Haines case wasn't exactly dynamite, but it had grown from a firecracker to a cherry bomb. If it exploded, the noise would be loud. And even a cherry bomb can cause injury if one gets too close.

"The Haines case is ready for the grand jury," announced Magnolia Young, assistant district attorney. "We have a motive, we have the opportunity and we have the victim."

Young was an athletic-looking woman of 33, not surprising, given that she coached a local girl's soccer team and had played the sport in college. She had short, straight hair and the tanned look of someone who spent time outside. She wore no makeup. When she moved her head, her shoulders moved at the same time, giving her a strangely Frankenstein manner that gave her the look of authority when she moved about. Her speech was always punchy and direct, just like her instructions to her soccer players. Juries knew what to do when they heard her instructions.

Magnolia Young wanted William Magowan to become Mississippi's next attorney general. For then, she could campaign to become the area's first female district attorney. The Haines case could do it for her.

"What about witnesses?" asked Magowan, now leaning back in his chair at the head of the conference table.

"The witness list includes the medical examiner who did the autopsy, the ambulance attendants who arrived on the scene, the police officer who processed the crime scene, a neighbor who heard them arguing the night before, Dr. Haines' nurse who said that she heard him say he wished he had never married her, and Dr. Haines himself," she said touching a finger with her thumb each time she stated a name.

"What if Dr. Haines refuses to testify?" asked Magowan.

"He'll have to testify," replied Young. "Most people in town have already convicted him in their minds. The only way he can get any sympathy is to take the witness stand."

"Besides," said one of the other attorneys at the table. "He killed her."

"Why am I nervous about this case?" asked the district attorney, leaning forward and tapping his fingers on the table.

There was silence as each of his assistants lowered their heads and looked at each other. Finally, Magnolia Young said what they were all thinking. "Because you're in a political race."

"That's what I thought too," he said. "But there is something about this case that isn't right. Something's missing."

"Do you think we lack evidence?" said one of the attorneys.

"I suppose we have tried cases with less evidence," he said. "But something doesn't feel right."

"William," said Young, immediately regretting calling the district attorney by his first name in front of the other two lawyers. "Trust me. If I thought there was major political risk for you I wouldn't recommend we move on this case. But I think just the opposite. Prosecuting this case will show that you are not afraid to tackle the difficult cases. People will admire you for that."

"What do the rest of you think?" asked Magowan with a lowered chin and raised eyebrow look to the two others.

"I say go," said one.

"And I say no."

Stephen Seger's comment caught them by surprise. Normally a quiet, efficient assistant, he was usually deferential in these meetings. He seldom spoke up, instead agreeing to do whatever the others wanted. Out of law school only two years, he was still learning the ropes. Single and clean-cut, he did what he was told. He had worked in the D.A.'s Office only six months and thus far had only handled property crimes, such as burglaries and grand larcenies. He was, in appearance and manner, the Clark Kent of the office.

"Go ahead," said Magowan.

"Sir, even if you win in court, you lose politically," said Seger. "As the case goes on, it will become more controversial. The trial will be reported every day in the newspaper. People will start taking sides. Magnolia is right about people thinking that Doc did it. But that will begin to change. Even though Doc has changed in demeanor, plenty of people in Corinth think he's a great man. Sooner or later, the question will be asked about why he is being prosecuted. And the answer will be that you are running for office. I think that the case should be delayed. There's nothing to lose by holding off on an indictment for another few months. You can say that more tests are being conducted."

"He makes a good point," said Magowan to Young.

"It's your call," she said.

The district attorney stood up. As he did so, the others followed suit. "I'll think it over and let you know tomorrow." He left the room, heading for the campaign trail.

Chapter 6

Most towns have a gathering place where everybody who knows everybody else meets to talk about everybody else. Old-timers especially like to meet there to socialize and gossip. More often than not, such a place is a restaurant in the downtown area.

Corinth, Mississippi is no exception to this phenomenon. Its downtown morning gathering place is Martha's Menu, an establishment that a newcomer might miss if he did not pay attention. Of course, the observant newcomer would notice an unusually high number of automobiles parked diagonally on the street and the smell of breakfast in the air. Located not quite mid-block on Cruise Street, the façade and inconspicuous sign of Martha's might lead one to believe that a one-room café resides on the other side of the door. Instead, upon passing through the entryway one gets the sensation of being inside the hands of a young child with clasped hands, turning them over to reveal eight little fingers accompanying a rhyme that goes, "Here is the church and here is the steeple, open the door and see all the people."

Morning is also the noisiest time at Martha's, when the clatter of cups, saucers and plates competes with the din of conversation from the regular customers. If one listens carefully, through the noise can be heard such enlightened phrases as: "Did you hear that . . ." "What do you think about what happened to . . ." and "Let me tell you what I heard. . . ."

There are two seating sections at Martha's, one up front where the smoke hangs thick and hazy, and one in the back, which is a little more upscale and, some would say, more refined. Others would simply opine that people who like biscuits, grits and bacon choose the front, while those who dine on omelettes and ham prefer the rear. Still others say that it doesn't make any difference because it's still pig and chicken products when all is said and done.

Sylvia Haines McChester and Sadie Haines Kellog, two of Dr. Marlin Haines' three sisters, sat rigid and

proper at a table against the wall in the rear section of the restaurant. Sylvia was 67, the oldest of the four Haines children. She had moved away from Corinth at age 20 to California in search of excitement. She waited on tables at a fine restaurant in the Gas Light district in downtown San Diego at night while attending nursing school during the day. She never found the doctor she was looking for. Just when she thought one was about to propose he would call off their relationship. It happened twice. Both times, she was told that she was too much woman. She thought it was a compliment until she was told that she was too domineering. She settled for a chef at a suburban country club, and for years their life together was tolerable, no doubt aided by the fact that she worked the day shift at the county hospital and he worked the dinner shift at the club. After ten years she volunteered for the midnight shift because the differential in pay was enticing and she found that being around her husband was disgusting. He had gained 40 pounds since their wedding day and had a pot belly that drooped over his belt buckle. He also had a drinking problem and another woman who wanted to know why she couldn't see him during the day anymore. Sylvia divorced him and moved back to Corinth 17 years ago, bringing with her a California accent and a carload of regrets, wondering what a life in California married to a rich doctor would have been like.

Sadie was 63 and still recovering from the death of

her husband just over two years ago. Sadie was known around town for her "Third Thursday Tea Parties," as they were called. Prim and proper, she existed for the tea parties and the accompanying social status. Her worst fear had been that upon the death of her husband she would be relegated to a minor role in Corinth's social scene, but such a situation had not occurred. Sylvia had pointed out rather bluntly only a few weeks ago that half the women who attended her teas were also widows. "Hell, Sadie, you're all hanging onto to each other like children. Get a real life," Sylvia had told her. Sadie reminded Sylvia that these were her friends and that the club was open to new members from time to time if Sylvia would like to join.

A waitress approached the Haines sisters' table and said, "There's a man who says he's here to meet you, ladies."

"By all means, bring him on back."

Sadie raised her napkin to her mouth and fidgeted. "I'm not sure this is a good idea," she said. "We don't even know this man."

"He's here to help Marlin," said Sylvia. "I'll do all the talking."

After being shown to the table, Jack Boulder, dressed in his usual khaki chinos and polo shirt, introduced himself. The waitress returned for their order. Boulder and Sadie ordered coffee.

"I'll have a cup of boiling water," said Sylvia, reaching down into her purse and extracting a small green and gold package of green tea, which she set in front of her. The waitress raised her eyes toward the ceiling as if to say "We get all kinds," then turned and left.

"Sylvia is into health and nutrition," Sadie announced softly. "But wait till you meet Sally. She's a genuine herbalist. You ask her about any vitamin and she can tell you everything. She fixed me up with a combination that keeps me feeling like I'm ten years younger." Boulder nodded and Sadie continued. "I hate that you had to come to Corinth under such circumstances," she said, already ignoring her older sister's admonition. "I was hoping you would say that you had come for the Slugburger Festival."

"The Slugburger Festival?" asked Boulder with a puzzled look.

"Oh, yes," replied Sadie. "It's our annual street party, Corinth reunion, and arts and craft show all rolled into one. And they always have a big name entertainer."

"What's a Slugburger?" asked Boulder.

"Well," said Sadie, with a turn of her chin. "During the war—the war to end all wars, you know, not that Yankee-Confederate thing—meat was in short supply and . . ."

"Don't tell me," said Boulder.

"It's not what you think. Meat was in short supply so someone came up with a patty that replaced hamburger meat. It is basically made with soy and is chock full of protein. Anyway, after the war, people just kept on eating them and today they are Corinth's little gift to the world. You need to eat one before you go back to Jackson. Better yet, stay for the Slugburger Festival."

"Do you investigate many cases like this, Mr. Boulder?" interjected Sylvia.

"What do you mean?"

"Where somebody gets framed," injected Sadie. Sylvia glared at her. Sadie tightened her lips and lowered her head.

"It's not a common occurrence," said Boulder.

"You said you wanted to learn more about our brother," said Sylvia. "What would you like to know?"

"First, I'd like to know more about his wife," said Boulder.

"You mean that awful creature he found in Florida," injected Sadie, then proffered a demure smile.

"I take it you didn't approve of her."

"That's putting it mildly," replied Sylvia. "She destroyed Marlin. I just hope he can recover from this."

The waitress returned with their orders. Boulder took a sip of his black coffee, Sadie dumped several teaspoons of sugar and a shot of milk into her coffee, and Sylvia began dipping a tea bag in her cup of hot water.

"How did she destroy him?"

"She smothered him," said Sylvia. "Wanted him home all the time. Jealous of everything he did. She was a very insecure person. Marlin couldn't go outside the house without her permission. And SHE always stayed inside. Painting her toenails and eating banana pudding."

"Eating banana pudding?"

"She was addicted to it," added Sadie with a nod. "She told Marlin that she had eaten banana pudding only once in her life and had gotten sick on it. Threw up in class after lunch in junior high school. Well, she got to Corinth, had some of Ester Wackerman's banana pudding and got addicted to it."

Boulder's head remained in place toward Sadie, but his eyes shifted to Sylvia seeking to confirm that his leg was not being pulled.

"She's right," said Sylvia. "The first week she and Marlin returned to Corinth, Marlin's neighbor, Ester, took over some of her banana pudding. Sadie, hand me that spoon. The new wife raved about it so much that other people began to send banana pudding."

"Ester told us about it at my Third Thursday group," said Sadie proudly. "So the members sent their banana puddings to Marlin's house. Finally, she got Ester's recipe. She gained 40 pounds. Then she told Marlin she couldn't be seen in public until she lost weight. He bought her every kind of weight loss program and machine on the market."

"Did she lose any weight?" asked Boulder.

"Are you kidding?" replied Sadie. "She just kept on

eating banana pudding. She was a sick person, I tell you."

"I understand she had a problem with headaches."

"That's what she says," said Sylvia. "I think she just wanted attention."

"And Sylvia should know," said Sadie. "She's a nurse."

"Oh, really," acknowledged Boulder.

"A retired one," she said in a low voice.

"She's a writer now," said Sadie proudly. "She writes articles for nursing magazines."

There was a pregnant pause while each of them took a sip from their cups. Then Sadie spoke up. "Marlin's in trouble, isn't he?"

"There is a strong possibility that he will be charged with murder."

"He didn't kill her," said Sylvia firmly.

"Who did?"

"She committed suicide," said Sylvia. "She wanted to go back to Florida, but Marlin wouldn't go. He's from Corinth and he will always live in Corinth. He loves this place. She didn't have any other way out. It's a sad story, but she is—well, was—a sad, sick person. Marlin couldn't kill anybody. He has spent his whole life keeping people alive and well."

They continued their conversation for 35 more minutes and three more cups of coffee and tea. Boulder didn't learn anything that he felt was pertinent to the case.

Dr. Marlin Haines was a well-respected man who married a trophy wife, brought her back to his home town and suffered from her insecurities and idiosyncrasies. He had seen men kill wives for less; he had seen women kill themselves for less. Maybe there was more evidence that pointed to a suicide. It was time to talk to the police officer who was on the scene.

Chapter 7

Officer Thomas "Tom-Tom" Thompson, Corinth Police Department, knew it wouldn't be much longer before the private eye from Jackson would be contacting him. Thompson worked the day shift and his patrol area included downtown Corinth and the surrounding area. There wasn't much that went on that he didn't know about.

Unlike most police officers, he liked to park his police car and get out on foot to get to know the citizens. Three years ago he graduated from the University of Southern Mississippi with a degree in criminal justice. The highlight of his college career had been a month-long semester in London where he worked with and studied the British constable. The attitude there about the police was different than that in America. Citizens respected the police more and became more involved with their work. The bobbies carried whistles and blew them when help was needed. When citizens heard the whistle, they came to the aid of the policemen. In America, citizens carry whistles and blow them to call for the police. Thompson learned in London that the best police officers got out on foot, mingled with the business people and observed what was normal activity. When something was abnormal, such a police officer would know about it. Downtown business owners and residents liked the tall, red-haired, freckle-faced

Thompson. He looked like Tom Sawyer grown up and had a personality to match.

Even with Thompson's keen sense of observation it didn't take a trained observer to notice that a showroom-new 1968 Camaro was in town. It took Thompson only a few inquiries to learn that it was driven by a private investigator who had been hired by Pace McHatten, and it took only logical deduction to know that his visit was about the death of Melanie Haines. So, at 10:00 a.m. when he pulled his patrol car into the police station parking lot and saw the Camaro parked in one of the visitor parking spots, he was not surprised at all. As he walked in the station's side door the desk sergeant motioned with his thumb and shouted at him. "Hey, Thompson. Visitor up front."

As Thompson entered the lobby, Jack Boulder stood and introduced himself. He didn't hold out his hand in a handshake, knowing police officers were naturally suspicious when someone used that gesture. Boulder told him why he was in Corinth and who had hired him. Did Thompson mind sharing some information about the case?

"Come on back to the interview room," replied Thompson.

They went to a small conference room in the back of the building. A table with four chairs comprised the only furniture in the room. There was a wire-reinforced, heavy-glass window on the back wall. On the side walls were framed uniformed patches from police departments around the country. Boulder walked over to one wall and studied a few.

"That one sure is familiar," said Boulder, pointing to the shoulder patch of the St. Louis Police Department.

"Why is that?" asked Thompson.

"I put in 20 years there," replied Boulder.

That was all it took. They spent the next ten minutes talking about police work in general and about St. Louis and Corinth in particular. In short, they established the link that binds the brotherhood of police officers no matter where they work. Thompson was eager to cooperate in the case at hand.

"I was on patrol when I got the call dispatching me to Dr. Haines' house. When I arrived, the ambulance was already there. Dr. Haines' wife was still on the floor and the paramedics were working on her hard, but it was obvious she was already gone. She had that blue-gray color."

"What was Dr. Haines doing?"

"He just stood there watching. I could tell he was concerned. He didn't look well at all. But he let the EMTs do the work."

"Do you remember anything about the room? Anything on the counter?" asked Boulder.

"I knew that would be asked," said the officer. "Hold on. " He got up and walked out of the room, returning immediately with a file folder, which he laid on the table and opened. "Here are the prints from the roll of film I shot."

Boulder picked them up and studied them. They were in color and covered every bit of space in the room except the ceiling. Boulder was impressed with the quality of work. They showed a large overturned bottle of pills on the kitchen counter. In the sink were two white bowls, each with yellow food stains. Lying inside one was a large spoon. Another bowl, the size of a cereal bowl, was on the counter. It was yellow with a blue ring around the top lip. There was a spoon inside it. Boulder wondered where Dr. Haines placed his cereal bowl. Probably in the dishwasher. A four-cup, drip coffeemaker was in the "on" position, its orange light glowing. The glass pot itself was half-full of coffee. There was a stack of envelopes, mostly bills, on the kitchen table. Otherwise, everything looked in its place.

"Did you notice a coffee cup?" asked Boulder.

"No. Everything that was there when I arrived is in those photographs. Except the people, of course."

"Did you photograph any other rooms in the house?"

"No," said Officer Thompson, dragging out the word. "I probably should have, but this looked like an accidental death at the time, so I just did the kitchen. Actually, I wasn't even required to do that in a case like this."

"You did very well," said Boulder. "This is very helpful. What did Dr. Haines say at the time?"

"Not much. He looked to be in shock to me. Several times he said 'Oh, Melanie, no—oh, Melanie, no'."

"Was there any other investigation?"

"Not by our department," said Thompson. "When the autopsy came back showing that she had an overdose we turned it over to the district attorney's office."

"I see. What's your gut feeling on this case?" asked Boulder.

"I could be wrong," said the officer. "But it sure looks like a suicide to me. I can't imagine Doc Haines killing anybody. He is a good man."

"Was there a suicide note?"

"I couldn't find one in the kitchen. Didn't search the rest of the place."

"So why is the district attorney thinking about charging Dr. Haines with murder?" asked Boulder.

Thompson leaned forward and chose his words carefully. "You had breakfast at Martha's Menu?"

"Yes," said Boulder, admiring the officer's police skills. "Did you see a movie theater across the street?"

"As a matter of fact, I think I did," said Boulder. "It had a painted sign on it. An old soft drink sign of some kind?"

"Are you in a hurry?" asked the police officer.

"Not really."

"Let's ride downtown."

They went outside and got into the patrol car. As they approached Martha's Menu on Cruise Street they pulled over into a loading zone and stopped. Officer Thompson pointed to the side of a large, dark brick building. On its side was a sign that read "Sin alco."

"I've never heard of that brand," remarked Boulder.

"I can't find anyone in Corinth who has heard of it either. That's the coliseum building." He shifted his position and pointed at a storefront across the street. "See that building that has the numbers above the door?"

"Sure."

"Any idea what's inside?"

"Looks like a little arts and crafts shop."

"Let's go inside," said Thompson. "I want you to see something."

They walked in and a middle-aged woman who looked like a model for a life insurance commercial walked toward them. "Hi, Tom-Tom," she said with a smile. "What can I do for you?"

"Would you mind if I showed off the theater?" asked Officer Thompson.

"Of course not. Be my guest. You know the way," she said, standing aside so that they could pass.

Thompson led them through the back storeroom of the shop and out another door that opened into a dark, cavernous room. As their eyes adjusted to the dim light, Boulder was astounded to see that the arts and crafts store had been built inside a theater. There were no seats, but there was a stage and a curtain with a gold

letter "P" in elegant script. It must have seated 300 people as a theater. There was even a balcony. Officer Thompson opened the door to the storeroom and they went back into the arts and crafts store.

"Hey Gracie, do you still have that document with the history of this place?" shouted Thompson toward the front of the store.

In less than a moment the woman brought a framed, two-page letter and handed it to the police officer. He handed it to Boulder and said, "Read this. You might find it interesting." Boulder took it and the other two went back to the front of the shop. Boulder leaned against a counter and read the document.

A Brief History of the Pickwick Theater
603-605 Cruise Street

The old Pickwick Theater began life in 1913 when B.F. Liddon designed and built the building to be used as a theater, which he named *The Gem*. The building was about 30 feet wide and 92½ feet long with a marquee over the sidewalk. An old picture shows the theater sign hanging between the windows of the second floor, with the name GEM, and the sign was in the shape of a crescent moon.

Legend has it that Mr. Liddon's daughter, Norrine, went to the Elite Theater with a dime for a ticket, but returned home in tears because the price was 15 cents. Mr. Liddon then built the Gem Theater in 1913, with an

admission price of 5 cents. The first day's income was a little more than $12.00—about 250 tickets. Mr. Liddon always kept admission prices low so everyone could afford a ticket, and often passed in children who did not have the money for a ticket.

On the first floor were about 300 seats, with a ladies restroom and storage room on the second floor, and balcony with about 150 seats, and in the top was the projection room. The stage and screen were formed by a large arch with a fancy plaster border and velvet curtains. In front of the stage were two very large radiators for heat in the winter (two other radiators were near the front door). In the ceiling above the stage were two large fans which pulled in cool air—this, of course, was in the era of silent movies when a player piano provided the only sound.

By 1923, Mr. Liddon had begun construction of the 1,000 seat Coliseum Theater which was opened July 4, 1924. The Gem was not needed in Corinth, so Mr. Liddon converted the theater into a store building. John and Jordan Timlake operated a heating and plumbing business there for a while, then Mr. Charles Mitchell and his father opened a dry goods store.

By 1935, Pickwick Dam was under construction and large numbers of workers moved to the Corinth area, so Mr. Liddon decided to reopen the Gem Theater under the name of the Pickwick Theater. He put back the sloping floor and bought new seats, installed a new cooling system which was quiet enough for the movies with sound, and cooled by a large sprayer system which drew in fresh air through the water spray. The front of the building was remodeled to show a new marquee with flashing neon lights over the Pickwick name. There were about 60 15-watt light bulbs placed under the marquee, and black architectural glass with green accent around the ticket office and poster frames.

The Pickwick Theater operated Monday through Friday from 1:00 p.m. till about 10:00 p.m. and from 10:00 a.m. till about 10:00 p.m. on Saturdays. Mr. Liddon never operated his theaters on Sunday. Admission was 10 cents until the World War II taxes raised it to 14 cents, then it went to 15 cents.

By the late 1950s, most people had TV sets and this caused a steady decline in movie attendance, and the Pickwick closed in the summer of 1961.

In 1962, the theater was remodeled into two store fronts with plate glass windows. Mr. and Mrs. Perry Clark operated a busy newsstand at 603 Cruise for a number of years, and Mrs Clara North operated a shoe store and shoe repair shop until she retired a few months ago at 605 Cruise St.

Boulder laid it down on the counter and went back into the open theater again. He stood there, head raised, taking it all in. He noticed that the stage wasn't very deep, which should have been obvious since this was a movie theater. After savoring the history of it for another moment he went back inside the shop and retrieved Officer Thompson.

As they emerged back onto the sidewalk on Cruise Street, Officer Thompson, said, "I guess you're wondering why I showed you all of that."

"You might say that," replied Boulder.

"Well, you see the front of this building looks one way, but inside is a different thing altogether."

"In other words, what you see isn't always what you get."

"That's right. And I think that's what is happening in the Dr. Haines case. We've got a good D.A. here, but politics is making the inside and the outside quite different."

Chapter 8

Boulder strolled down Fillmore Street, heading back to McHatten's office. Still mentally processing his meeting with the sisters, he turned the corner onto Waldron Street and approached the courthouse square. Walking the final block toward McHatten's office, he decided to stop at the drug store up ahead and purchase a roll of antacid tablets. The heavy breakfast at the Generals' Quarters and several cups of coffee were already taking their toll. He walked inside and discovered a drug store like drug stores should be. There was a soda fountain on the right hand side, a counter along the wall on the left side and a pharmacy in the rear. There was also a seating area. Boulder had discovered Borroum's Drug Store. The man behind the counter wearing a pharmacist's smock looked familiar. Could it be?

"Excuse me," said Boulder. "Are you Kenny Bartley?"

It was one of Boulder's pals from high school. He was about 20 pounds heavier, but was otherwise a mature version of the boy Boulder remembered.

"My gosh! Jack Boulder!" Just then, the telephone behind the counter rang. Bartley picked up the receiver with his left hand and raised his right index finger in the "wait a minute" sign. "Yes, of course," Bartley said to the telephone nodding. After a half-minute he held the phone out from his ear and handed Boulder a piece of paper. "Read this," he whispered. "This might take a few minutes."

Boulder nodded affirmatively and took a seat at the soda fountain on the opposite side of the store. He ordered a soft drink and began reading.

The history of this store begins as a war ends. Dr. Andrew Jackson (Jack) Borroum had just been released from a northern prison camp and mustered out of the Army at Atlanta, Georgia. He had worked for the northern armies when he was captured and the southern armies when he was free. With no particular idea in mind except to go home, he started toward Oxford, Mississippi on horseback. On his way, he stopped in Corinth and met a Dr. Young, whom he had known before. Dr. Young convinced him to stay and practice with him. That he did, opening his office almost immediately. Corinth was still under military rule at the time.

Dr. Borroum began to dispense medicines, having to make most of them. Soon he decided to open a drug store that would be both wholesale and retail, as Corinth did not have one at that time. The store was first located at #4 Front Street, now called Cruise Street, and beside where Corinth Water and Gas is today. Later it was moved to its present location of 604 Waldron Street when the courthouse was built. The present building was built around 1843 and was originally a tannery, with a livery stable next door. The walls are hand-made brick, and are four bricks thick.

Always the center of activity, it was like a general store in that it carried a variety of merchandise, such as perfumes, incense, drugs, herbs, tobacco, and coffee, as each became available. As Dr. Borroum's books reveal, he was often paid in vegetables, eggs and chickens. His records do not show an account closed except on the death of a customer. In one way or another, he accepted any kind of payment, and all the accounts are marked "paid."

Dr. Borroum also published a paper, "Dr. A. J. Borroum's Courier." It would give information on the newest medicines and the arrival of fresh herbs and new merchandise. There would also be poems, short stories, anecdotes, jokes and tales related to the time of year it was published. Of course, it also advertised the drug store.

Dr. Borroum continued his medical practice and the operating of the drug store for 32 years, his sons joining him as they finished their medical training. Upon his death, his oldest son, Dr. James Alexis (Lex) Borroum became the sole owner of the store. It continued as a wholesale-retail operation until the late 1920s.

Dr. Lex differed from his father in that he had a great interest in politics. He was also an animal lover and raised canaries in the back of the store building. His interest in politics made the store a great place to be on election night in Corinth. A scoreboard was maintained on the windows until the last vote was in. The men would spin many a yarn and swap many dollars as friendly bets were won and lost. Many of Mississippi's governors began their campaigns in Corinth by always coming by the store and seeing how "the feeling was" as they talked to customers and Dr. Borroum.

Being a border town on the Mississippi-Tennessee line, Corinth was a hub for marriages because Mississippi marriage laws were much more lenient than those of surrounding states. It was quite customary for the justices of the peace to use the back of the store to marry people after regular courthouse hours.

After Dr. Lex's death in 1932, Dr. A. J. Borroum's second-oldest son, Conrad, and Conrad's wife, Cristle, along with mother Willou, operated the drug store. About five years later, Conrad went to work for the Tennessee Valley Authority, leaving Dr. Borroum's youngest son, Col. James Lannes Borroum and his wife, Loretta, to run the store with Willou. The store was modernized in the late 1930s and a soda fountain, booths and tables, and a juke box were added.

With the arrival of the "chain store era," a decision had to be made. The family decided that the store would remain the same, offering the services it had for a hundred years such as charge accounts without service charges, free delivery, and free gift wrapping. It also offers free blood pressure checks, and was the first store in the area to offer senior citizen discounts. Another plus is the personal shopping service to elderly customers and those either too sick or otherwise too incapacitated to come to the store.

The store has a museum area where some of the original cobalt blue dispensing bottles with gold leaf labels and medicinal names written in Latin are displayed along with pharmaceutical scales with amethyst balances, medicines and other antique paraphernalia, including a tiny mid-wife spoon. There is also a large Indian artifact collection on display that was personally collected by Col. Lannes Borroum and a Civil War collection of artifacts assembled by Col. Borroum and his brother, Conrad. In this collection hang the sword and scabbard and powder horn of Jessie Kilgore Borroum, Dr. Jack Borroum's brother who was killed in the Battle of Atlanta.

The store today features a modern pharmacy operated by Camille Borroum Mitchell, daughter of Col. Jack Borroum and Corinth's first woman pharmacist. She has practiced pharmacy for 47 years. The said fountain is still the center of things and is kept in operation by Camille's oldest son, Lex. It has everything from real malted milks to ice cream sodas.

There is also a large tobacconist shop operated by Bo, Camille's oldest son and Dr. Jack Borroum's great, great grandson. The tobacco mixes are special blends he has made, and sport such names as Bo's Trash, Borroum's Blend and Kimmons Old Fashion. There is also a wide selection of imported teas and coffees.

The candy shop, which is operated by Lex and his wife, Debbi, sells fine chocolates by the piece, by the pound or by specially packaged boxes. There is also salt water taffy, gourmet jelly beans, hand-made "licken sticks," the "all-day" suckers, and hand-dipped pretzels. They also have roasted nuts, sesame sticks and sunflower seeds.

The original wall cases have been put in place and restored. The old prescription counter was also restored, and the 1926 cash register has been reconditioned.

The store has survived the changes of time since its

establishment in 1865. It is the oldest continuously operating drug store in Mississippi. It is operated by the sixth generation of Dr. Andrew Jackson Borroum. Efforts are underway to have the pharmacy placed in the National Register of Historic Places.

Just as Boulder finished reading, he saw his old schoolmate hanging up the telephone receiver. Bartley came from around the counter and they shook hands, then hugged. "What in the world are you doing in Corinth?" asked Bartley.

"I might ask you the same thing," said Boulder. "It's been over 20 years since we were seniors at Central High School in Jackson."

"I moved up here about 5 years ago," he said. "My wife is from these parts and wanted to get back home."

"So you're a pharmacist now?"

"You got it. And what are you doing here?"

"Do you know Dr. Haines?" asked Boulder.

"Of course. Everybody knows Dr. Haines."

Boulder gave his high school classmate the short version of his career, concluding with the fact that he was now a private investigator hired by Dr. Haines' attorney. "Anything you can help me with about the case?"

"Are they still are saying she died from acetaminophen poisoning?" asked the pharmacist.

"That's what I understand."

"I'm not saying that couldn't happen," he said intently. "But it just doesn't make a whole lot of sense."

"Excuse me, young man," said an old lady who must have been in her 70s, standing behind Boulder. "I hate to interrupt, but I need my prescription filled."

"Excuse me, Jack," said Bartley. "Can you come back later this afternoon? I need to take care of our customers."

Boulder said that would be no problem, then headed for the door. Anyway, it was almost time to interview Sally Haines.

Chapter 9

The sign on the base of the statue of the life-sized lion read Gilmore's, a new sign to go with a new building that contained a pro shop and restaurant, all surrounded by tennis courts, a golf course and a new upscale residential development.

Jack Boulder glanced at the lion as he walked by it. He went inside and was seated at a table for four in the center of the room. It was high noon and all he wanted was a large glass of ice water, something that was not on the menu. His request was promptly accommodated by a waitress who looked like a high school senior working for the summer. She even added a twist of lemon. Boulder gulped half the glass of water down at once.

At the next table an aristocratic gentleman in golf attire grinned and said, "Nothing like a glass of ice water on a hot day."

"No kidding."

"Are you from Corinth?" the man asked.

"No, just here on business for a few days," said Boulder. He wanted to get the attention off himself. "I noticed a statue of a lion out front."

"Oh, yeah," said the man with a smile. "That's Gilmore."

"Oh," replied Boulder.

"You ever heard of Roscoe Turner?" asked the man.

"Can't say that I have."

"Ever heard of *Time* magazine?" he continued.

"Sure."

"Well, Roscoe Turner was once on the cover of *Time* magazine," said the man. "To my mind he's the most famous person who ever came from Corinth."

"You don't say."

"Even people around here don't know the whole story about Roscoe Turner. He was something else, I tell you."

Obviously, the man was going to tell the story, so Boulder said, "Tell me about him." And for the next 20 minutes, he did.

Roscoe Turner was born in Corinth in 1895. He learned to fly while stationed in Europe at the end of World War I. After the war he and a fellow pilot started a flying circus, traveling all over the South in a Canadian-built Jenny. In those days a county fair, circus or carnival was not complete without an airplane. Turner did the flying and his partner did the wing-walking and parachuting. After the show, Turner took people up for rides in the airplane. During this period, Turner learned the value of self-promotion. He had a custom-made uniform that included diamond-studded wings with his initials on them, polished riding boots, a Sam Browne belt, and beige officer-style hat. He topped it off with a mustache waxed into needle-fine points and a movie star smile.

He staged his first air show in Corinth in 1922 just

before Christmas. About that time, S. H. Curlee, a millionaire clothier from Corinth, hired Turner to fly salespersons to distant towns to advertise Curlee clothes. When he wasn't flying salesmen, he was barnstorming. Turner met Igor Sikorsky, a Russian-born aircraft designer who had moved to the United States and had built the S-29A, the largest commercial plane in the country at that time. It carried 14 passengers in an enclosed cabin, and the pilot operated it from an open cockpit. Turner bought the plane from Sikorsky and sold his services for advertising and charter flights, continuing to benefit from his promotional skills. He met many national personalities and even carried Will Rogers on the first cross-country flight the famous humorist ever made. When he wasn't flying, he was speaking at civic clubs and public gatherings advocating the building of airports, encouraging the development of airlines, and predicting things to come in the world of aviation.

Turner's "opportunity of a lifetime" presented itself when a brash, young movie producer named Howard Hughes contracted Turner to fly his S-29A in an epic World War I film called *Hell's Angels*. The final scene was to be the downing of a German Gotha bomber. The S-29A was painted to look like the bomber. During filming, the movie had a blast of publicity and Turner became more well-known as he flew the plane in a number of scenes. Hughes asked Turner to put the plane in a spin to simulate the beginning of its crash, but Turner refused until the aging plane was checked by a mechanic. While Turner was away from the field another pilot was offered $1,000 to put the plane in a spin for the cameras and a mechanic was offered $100 to operate smoke equipment from the cabin. When the pilot put the plane in a spin he thought the wing was breaking, so he jumped from the open cockpit, yelling to the mechanic to bail out. Unfortunately, the plane crashed with the mechanic aboard. The movie was released in 1930, but Turner was out of business because of the loss of the plane.

It wasn't long before Turner was flying as a test pilot, then a pilot for a small startup airline. Eventually, he persuaded the president of Gilmore Oil Company to buy a Lockheed Air Express so that Turner could fly it and promote the company's Red Lion oil products. The plane was christened the Red Lion by a movie starlet and Turner was sent out to set records and enter races. Ever the promoter, Turner adopted a real lion cub and took it with him everywhere he went. This, of course, led to more publicity. The cub was named "Gilmore" and outfitted with a parachute to satisfy the Humane Society. Larger parachutes were made as Gilmore grew in size. At hotels, Turner would register as "Roscoe Turner and Gilmore."

Roscoe Turner wasted no time in setting records. In 1930, he set a new east-west record and a Canada-

Mexico mark, with Gilmore also on board. In the early 1930s he entered numerous races and set many records as the public became more enthralled with dashing aviators. He and Jimmy Doolittle were the only pilots to win both the Bendix and Thompson trophies. International fame would come after he entered the MacRobertson London-to-Melbourne air race in 1934. He and his copilot came in second with an elapsed time of 3 days, 21 hours, 5 minutes and 2 seconds, and were the only Americans to complete the flight. Sixty-three aircraft had entered the race, 20 had started, and only 12 reached the final destination. He entered even more races and set more records. He preached the importance of a strong air force, and served as a consultant to the U.S. House of Representatives Science and Aeronautics Committee. Many honors came his way, including the Distinguished Flying Cross, one of only a few awarded to non-military pilots. The townspeople of Corinth named their airport after their most famous native son.

As for Gilmore, when he reached 150 pounds Turner had to leave him at home. Gilmore was placed on a California animal farm and his upkeep was paid for by Turner until the lion died in 1952 at the age of 22. Gilmore is preserved along with many of Turner's planes and other articles at the National Air and Space Museum's Garber facility. The plane that Turner flew in the Melbourne race was on display at the museum's Washington facility. Turner died in 1970.

"That's quite a story," said Boulder.

"And now you understand why there's a lion out there, and why this place is named Gilmore's."

Just then a woman with short, dark, perspiration-soaked hair wearing a white tennis outfit trimmed in lime green walked in and strode purposefully toward Boulder's table. He could not tell if she was looking at him or the table behind him. She walked up, stuck out a sweaty hand and said breathlessly, "Sorry I'm late. Our match went three sets."

"Not a problem," he said, standing up and thanking the other man for the information.

"Keep your seat. I need to get a shower. See that patio home sticking out over there across the driving range?" she said pointing toward a cluster of houses across the driving range. "Give me 15 minutes, then come on over. You can park in the front."

She swiveled around, then headed out the door, leaving Boulder to study her from behind. If she was in her 50s, she certainly didn't show it. Her tanned body was taut and one that women ten years younger envied.

Chapter 10

She opened the door and stood before him barefoot-ed, wearing a white terry cloth robe with the initials SHH on the breast pocket. In her right hand was a small glass of orange juice.

"Please come in," she said, stepping back. "You said you wanted to talk about Marlin? I guess Mac hired you, huh?"

He walked into a blue carpeted living room that featured a vaulted ceiling and a bar on the opposite side. Sliding glass doors led outside to a patio and a view of the fairway beyond. The walls were solid white. On the walls were framed paintings of sand dunes and sea oats. The feeling was beach resort condominium. She sat down in a white stuffed chair, he on the sofa.

"That's right," he said.

"Have you talked to my sisters?"

"This morning."

"What do they say?"

"That your brother succumbed to a greedy woman and is about to be indicted by a greedy politician."

"Good for them," she said. "Could not have said it better myself."

"You don't approve, I take it."

"Mr. Boulder, Marlin may be a prominent physician and he may become an accused murderer. But to me and my sisters, he's our brother. And nobody is going to take advantage of him or hurt him. The Haines girls have always stuck together."

"How often did you see your brother?"

"You make it sound like he's dead," she snapped. "I SEE my brother often."

"When was the last time?"

"I'm not sure. Three or four weeks ago."

"Did you see him regularly? Like every week or every month or something?"

"No," she said. "And unfortunately I don't see him enough. It's been getting hard to see him with her around."

"His wife?"

"Yes. The little witch from Florida."

Just then the sound of an alarm clock came from a room off the living room. She acted as if she didn't hear it. Boulder said, "Do you need to check that?"

"No. That's just my computer telling me I have an e-mail. It's probably just junk mail." She stood up. "Let me check it anyway just in case. Then I need to get dressed."

She walked from the living room to the other room. The sounds of someone tapping a keyboard and the clicking sound of one using a computer mouse could be heard. Then she was standing in the doorway.

"I'll be back in a moment. If you need something cold, the refrigerator should have everything you need."

She left and he heard a door shut where the bedroom

would be located. He went inside the room where the computer was located. It was a home office arrangement, much like Boulder's third bedroom in his condominium. He looked at the computer screen and noticed that it was still open to the mail manager setting. He stole a look down the hall, then reached down and clicked the arrow on the screen to "sent mail." A list of messages that had been sent appeared. There were four. One was to the Internet service provider, two others were to an on-line auction company and one was to "Sylvia1922@corinthnet.com." It was entitled, "Subject: The Recipe." He clicked on it and read:

Syl—here's the banana pudding recipe. Don't forget the most important ingredient.

1 vanilla instant pudding
2 c. milk
1 can sweetened condensed milk
1 package whipped topping
vanilla wafers
bananas
D. Angel mushrooms

Mix pudding, dried mushrooms and milk until thick. Add condensed milk and whipped topping. Layer bananas, cookies and pudding mixture.

He clicked the appropriate icons on the screen and returned the computer to its earlier setting. He walked back to living room and, as was his custom, studied the surrounding environment more closely. The magazines on the coffee table could be classified into three subject areas. The first was news magazines, the second was tennis publications and the third had to do with health issues, especially vitamins and herbal products. On a table against the wall near the front door was a 4x6-inch framed photo of Sally Haines and another woman in full military dress blues. She wore the rank of lieutenant colonel and the uniform was that of the United States Air Force. On the wall above was an Air Force certificate of commendation recognizing the efforts of Haines.

"Find anything interesting, Mr. Boulder?" came the voice from behind him. It was Sally Haines. She was wearing jeans and a tee shirt that said "Slugburger Festival" on it.

"I did. I didn't know you were in the military."

"I was," she said. "Retired three years ago. Moved back home like so many Mississippians."

"Are you working now?" he asked.

"Teach part-time at the community college and play tennis the rest of the time."

"I understand you are the youngest of the four children?" he said, raising his voice at the end to make it a question.

"Right. Sylvia is the oldest, then Marlin, then Sadie

and then me. Sylvia is two years older than Marlin, Sadie four years younger, and I'm eight years younger than Sadie. By the time I was ten years old, they were all grown and gone."

"Were you close to your brother?"

"All things considered, I would say so," she said. "We were not distant. Being in the military I wasn't home much. Still, we stayed in touch. We never missed a Thanksgiving together. That's true to this day. But my older sisters are closer to him. Always protected him. We used to say that the three of them were like a sandwich, with Sylvia and Sadie the bread and Marlin the meat. You couldn't get to him without going through them."

"What do you think about Melanie's death?"

"Looks like a suicide to me."

"When was the last time you were in their home?"

"Hmm," she said putting her hand to chin. "I guess it would have been about a month ago. He wanted me to witness his will."

"He changed his will?"

"He was always changing his will. And he always had me witness his signature. He would get it redone down at Pace McHatten's office, then call me."

"That sounds odd," said Boulder.

"McHatten goes through a lot of secretaries," she said. "Marlin said that when he died he wanted some-one who would be easy to locate if there were any problems. I've witnessed four new wills in three years."

"I guess McHatten couldn't be a witness since he drew it up," said Boulder. "Do you know anything about the contents of the will?"

"Even if I did, I wouldn't tell anybody," she said coldly. "This is my brother we're talking about."

"Right," said Boulder. He detected a chill in their conversation and decided to end it. "If you think of anything that can help Marlin, call me at the Generals' Quarters." She assured him that she would. They said goodbye and he left. As he pulled out of the driveway she picked up a telephone and dialed a number.

"Syl, he took the bait—just as planned."

Chapter 11

He drove directly downtown and parked in front of Borroum's Pharmacy. It was almost 2:30 p.m. Kenny Bartley was at the back of the counter behind the ornate cash register writing on a piece of paper. He looked up as Boulder approached.

"I'm in need of some pharmaceutical information," said Boulder.

"I'd say you have come to the right place," said Bartley, returning his pen to his shirt pocket. "Sorry I couldn't help you earlier, but customers come first here. Let's get a cup of coffee and sit down."

Boulder followed him across the floor to the counter where they ordered two cups of coffee. They went back to the rear of the store and settled in a booth against the wall.

"You know the cause of death of Melanie Haines?" asked Boulder, bringing them back to the point of their original conversation.

"Toxic reaction to acetaminophen."

"You said you doubted that. Why?" probed Boulder. "The doc said too much could kill a person. Isn't that true?"

"No doubt about it."

Boulder looked down at his coffee cup and turned it back and forth in the saucer. Kenny Bartley sensed his frustration.

"Jack, I know it's not very common, but it can happen," said the pharmacist.

"Did Dr. Haines buy any here in the store?"

"Heck, no. Like most physicians he had enough free samples of almost any pain reliever or drug on the market. No need for him to buy any here or anywhere else, for that matter."

"One more thing," said Boulder, still looking down. "If you were going to poison somebody and didn't want to get caught, how would you do it?" There was the sound of a sizzle on the grill behind the counter as a raw piece of hamburger was plopped on the hot surface.

"Oh, good question," he said with a grin.

"I take it you like this subject."

"I worked my way through pharmacy school at a regional crime lab. I was around pathologists all the time. We even had a toxicologist. They love the challenge of detecting a poisoning death. You really have to know what to look for." He was becoming animated as he talked, as if giving a lecture to a group of interested students and he was the guru of poison. "The thing about getting away with poisoning someone is getting them to take it when you're not around. After all, if you're around the victim and poisoning is suspected, then you become a suspect."

"So when someone is poisoned, it's usually by someone who has been with them?"

"Yes," said the pharmacist. "And it's usually the

spouse."

"That doesn't look good for Dr. Haines," said Boulder.

"I take the opposite position," said Bartley. "He's a doctor. If he was going to poison his wife, he would know that he would be the most logical suspect since he has access to various kinds of poisons. What I'm saying is that since he's a doctor he wouldn't choose poison."

"Unless he was desperate to get rid of her, and he wasn't reasoning at his normal capacity."

"You do have a good point there," said Bartley. "It's just that it's too obvious. I learned at the crime lab that when it's too obvious, some further investigation is needed."

"That's what I'm doing."

"Oh, I'm sorry," said Bartley. "I didn't mean to imply anything about your investigation. I'm glad they hired you. I'm just saying I don't think Dr. Haines did it."

"The question is still open. If you were going to poison somebody, what would you use?"

"I wouldn't use any of the old ones like arsenic and strychnine. They are easily detectable and can take a long time to go to work. Ricin is very deadly and hard to trace, but you would need someone who is a specialist to get a dose of that. Doc Haines isn't a specialist."

"His son is a doctor at a medical center in Houston,"

Boulder said seriously.

"Hmm," replied Bartley, then continued. "Succinyl choline is not detected very easily. It's rather deadly. That's what bow hunters use on the tips of their arrows. Carbon tetrachloride might be another possibility. Sometimes alchoholics drink household cleaners containing it. One would look in the liver for evidence of all this. The liver is a most amazing organ, Jack. It serves as the body's filter. It's as tough as can be until it breaks down. Then the rest of the body is in trouble." Bartley paused, taking a sip of the coffee in front of him. "Another angle is the use of natural ingredients. Tea made from mistletoe berries is deadly. Then, of course, there is always mushrooms," said Bartley.

Boulder's head almost jerked. "Mushrooms?" he asked, now remembering the electronic mail message on Sally Haines' computer.

"Sure," the pharmacist replied. "There are many kinds of poisonous mushrooms around. They grow wild in the woods. Any good scoutmaster knows which ones are poisonous. They can be very deadly. You may be interested to know that there are over 9,000 cases of mushroom poisoning reported every year in the U.S."

"Have you ever heard of—oh, wait a minute, I can't remember," said Boulder, struggling with his memory. "Have you ever heard of something called Heaven's mushrooms?"

Bartley placed his chin in his hand and said, "Nope,

that doesn't ring a bell."

"No! Not Heaven," exclaimed Boulder, then realizing he needed to keep his voice down. "Angel. Angel mushrooms."

"Ah," said Bartley. "An especially potent specimen. The Destroying Angel is very toxic and can kill a person if eaten. It's one of the *aminitas* group. The first symptom would probably be abdominal pain, followed by vomiting, then weakness. Do you think she may have eaten mushrooms?"

"I'm not sure, but there is a possibility."

"If the lab found a liver loaded with acetaminophen I doubt they would go much farther and test for mushrooms. A pathologist would really have to know what to look for. Mushrooms are not easily detectable and could be easily missed."

"Hmm," was all Boulder said, his mind now processing this new information. "I may need you for some more information if this develops."

"I'll be right here."

They stood up and shook hands, old high school friends reconnecting after many years in a most unexpected way. Funny, but neither had said a word about the old days. This case dominated their minds. Boulder promised he wouldn't leave town without stopping by to say goodbye.

"Oh, just one more thing," said Boulder. "Has anybody bought a large amount of acetaminophen in the last few weeks?"

Bartley thought a minute, then said, "Amy Mendenhall. She came in a couple of weeks ago and bought two 500-tablet bottles, then was back 15 minutes later to pick up one more bottle of the same size. I joked with her that Judge McHatten must have a big headache."

"Judge McHatten?"

"Yeah. Amy Mendenhall is Judge McHatten's secretary."

Chapter 12

Boulder walked down the street to McHatten's law office and found it locked up and dark inside. He looked at the watch on his wrist. It showed 4:15 p.m. Figuring that McHatten probably closed at four every day, Boulder decided to interview the neighbors around Dr. Haines' residence. He drove back to the Generals' Quarters, parked his car in the wide driveway facing Gloster Street, and walked back down Fillmore.

He walked past the Haines house and knocked on the door of the residence next to it. A man in his 40s wearing a khaki poplin suit and holding a briefcase opened the door. Boulder asked him if he could ask him a few questions about his neighbor, explaining that he had been hired by Dr. Haines' lawyer. The man invited him in.

"I just got in from work," the man said. "How can I help you?"

"I'm attempting to find out who might have visited the house on the day of Mrs. Haines' death," said Boulder.

"Can't help you there," said the man. "I was out of town on business that whole week. My wife was gone also. But if you want to know anything about anybody on this block, just go across Fillmore and talk to Miss Carolina Gilman. She sits on that front screen porch and watches everything. I don't see how she does it, as hot as it is."

Boulder thanked him and went across the street. The house was a one-story bungalow. The screen gave the appearance of a front porch with tinted glass on it. Sure enough, sitting on the front porch in a cane rocking chair under a whirling ceiling fan was a little old lady who looked like Granny on the Beverly Hillbillies television series. She had a high-pitched, nasalized voice to match the look. She also liked to talk.

"Marlin left the house in the morning, as usual," she said. "After that, there was a virtual parade of people in and out of that house. About 8:00 a.m., a young girl went in. Had a bowl of something covered up with a napkin, and a box, like a cereal box. She didn't stay five minutes. Next was Sadie Haines. That's Marlin's sister, you know. She had a picnic basket. She stayed almost an hour. Marlin came back at noon, and then the ambulance and the police and all kinds of commotion like I hadn't seen in many a spell."

Boulder talked to her for 20 minutes longer about Dr. Haines and his marriage to the young woman from Florida. She said that Marlin just didn't know what to do after Rosemary died and this young wife was just proof that he had gone crazy. She said that everybody knows that Marlin "put her to sleep," but who wouldn't have done the same thing in his place? The girl was, after all, a bossy little hussy who was after a rich old man. She would have killed him before long, for goodness sake.

The third visit was to the house on the other side of the Haines house. Boulder learned from a young housewife that at "about nine" a woman matching the description of Sadie Haines arrived at the house. She was sure it was nine because the *Today Show* was just ending. The housewife didn't know the Haines couple, even though they were neighbors. She and her husband had lived in Corinth for only a few weeks. Her husband had been transferred to town to work on *National Geographic* magazine, which was published in Corinth.

Boulder walked back to the Generals' Quarters and called Laura Webster, his girlfriend. It was now after 6:00 p.m., but he knew she probably would not be found at home. She answered on the second ring at her law office. He got right to the heart of the matter.

"What I know so far is that on the day of Melanie Haines' death, her husband, Marlin Haines, M.D., got up at his usual 5:30 a.m., had a bowl of cereal and went to his office as usual. Sometime between eight and nine Melanie was visited by a young woman carrying a covered bowl of something. At nine, Sadie Haines, the doc's sister, paid a visit and she was bearing a picnic basket. I presume that these visitors brought banana pudding."

"Why?"

He told her about Melanie's obsession for the pudding and about his interviews with Marlin's sisters. Then their conversation turned to the lawyer. He related the information about McHatten's secretary buying three large bottles of acetaminophen the day before the death. He also told her about the mushroom possibility.

"Sherlock," said Laura teasingly. "I would say that you have yourself a tangled web up there. It wouldn't be going too far to suggest that you may have a conspiracy in Corinth."

"Tomorrow I'm going to talk to the secretary first thing, then go to the police and the district attorney with what I have."

"Hold on a minute," she said. "Your police personality is beginning to show. Who's your client?"

"Pace McHatten."

"That's right," she said. "You might be an expert in criminal law, but the law of agency says that you have a duty to disclose any information you gain in the course of your employment to your client. I would encourage you to talk to him first."

"Even if he is a disgusting human being?"

"That's even more reason," she said. "Listen, you be careful up there. It sounds like you might be onto something. Meanwhile, I'll do some research here on poisonings and see if I can find anything."

Chapter 13

The next morning, Boulder walked into McHatten's office at 8:05 a.m. The reception room was the same as when he had seen it last, except for one thing. There was a new receptionist at the desk.

"What happened to Amy?" asked Boulder.

"She's no longer with the firm," said an efficient, middle-aged woman who looked and acted like a middle school substitute teacher. "How may I help you?" There was an extra emphasis on the word "I."

"I'm Jack Boulder. I'm a private investigator working for Mr. McHatten. Who are you?"

"The temp service sent me," she said. "I work where I'm needed."

"How can I get in touch with Amy?"

"Do you want to get in touch with Amy or do you want to see Judge McHatten?"

"If you can't tell me how to get in touch with Amy, then I'd like to see Mr. McHatten."

"One moment, please." She raised her left eyebrow, picked up the telephone, dialed a number and said, "Mr. Blunder is here to see you, sir." She looked at Boulder as if to say "Gotcha" then said, "You may go up now. Judge McHatten's office is at the top of the stairs."

Boulder ascended the stairs and entered McHatten's office. The "Judge" looked the same as he did the first time Boulder met him, right down to the seersucker suit.

It looked as if he had on the same clothes. Before McHatten could say anything, Boulder asked, "What happened to your other secretary?"

"Unfortunately, she found it necessary to seek other employment," he said with a dismissive tone.

"Why did you send her to buy three large bottles of acetaminophen for you on July seventeenth?"

"I had a headache," he said drily.

"You know," said Boulder, still standing. "It would be a shame if I had to go to the district attorney and tell him that my client bought the same type medicine that Dr. Haines' wife died from."

"Get out of here," he said, his voice rising. "I need someone who believes in the innocence of my client."

"Maybe you are right," said Boulder. "Because you certainly aren't interested in someone who is seeking the truth, are you?"

He turned and walked back downstairs and out the door. He walked across the street to the courthouse and found a public telephone. He looked in the book and found four Mendenhalls listed in Corinth. Two were male and two were female names. He called the first male name, remembering Amy's photo on the credenza. Amy answered on the first ring. A child was crying in the background. Boulder asked if he could come over and talk to her. She didn't mind at all.

Amy Mendenhall and her husband lived in a small frame house with a one-car carport two blocks from downtown. The section of town was not as nice as Dr. Haines' area, but it was clean and neat, and shouted blue collar America. A chain link fence encircled the front yard and near the sidewalk to the front door was a children's portable pool that held about eight inches of water. Toys were scattered around it. When Boulder arrived she invited him into the small living room that had family pictures on walls, on tops of furniture and in a photo album on the coffee table. There was a picture of Jesus on one wall. The room was cold from a noisy window air-conditioner. Amy wore a pair of light blue jeans and a tee shirt with a blue flame under which was written "Gas Gives You More For Your Money."

"Where's your son?" said Boulder, pointing to a photograph of her, a man and a small boy.

"He's next door at my mom's house."

"Where does your husband work?"

"He's a service rep at the gas company."

"I guess you know why I'm here," said Boulder.

"Not really."

"Why did you leave Mr. McHatten's employment?" asked Boulder. It felt good not to call him "Judge."

"I just didn't get along with him," she said. "He wanted me to work late, but I need to pick up Robbie at day care by 5:30. Plus, he's not the easiest man to get along with. He goes through a lot of secretaries. I guess I thought I could handle it."

"How long did you work for him?"

"About two months."

"Remember the day he sent you to Borroum's to get those bottles of pain reliever?"

"Oh, sure," she said.

"Did he say why he needed that much medicine?"

"I can't recall," she said. "He sent me on a lot of errands for things. I never asked."

"What about the day Dr. Haines called him after Mrs. Haines died? Did he seem any different?"

"Not really." she said. "I guess I'm not being much help."

"Last question: Did you give the pain medicine to Judge McHatten?"

"Yes," she said. "I brought it back to the office, took it upstairs and handed it to him. He told me thanks and put it in his bottom right hand desk drawer."

He thanked her, wished her well and drove away in his Camaro heading to the home of Sylvia Haines McChester.

Chapter 14

Sylvia McChester let the cold water from the shower head drench her shoulders and back. The last soapy bubbles rolled down her legs and into the drain. She reached down and twisted the faucet, turning off the shower. She stepped out of the tub and dried herself with a thirsty cotton towel. She decided to let her hair dry naturally today. Ten minutes later she was dressed in Bermuda shorts and a yellow cotton blouse, the perfect outfit for writing articles about ethics and nursing. She loved her life these days, so unlike what she had been through in California. She worked out of her apartment, faxing or e-mailing her articles in to health publications. She had never thought of herself as a writer. A reporter was more like it. In today's rapidly changing healthcare industry, her articles were in demand. Enough so that she could make a decent living at it.

Sylvia lived in the heart of downtown Corinth in a second-floor apartment above a jewelry store. She was one of the first residents in the downtown residential revitalization program spearheaded by the Corinth Downtown Association. Having lived in San Diego, she knew that downtown residential housing was not a fad, but a trend. She knew that before long, every upstairs space in downtown Corinth would be occupied by apartment-dwellers like herself.

Her apartment was a showplace. It had beautifully redone hardwood floors, exposed brick interior walls, and a ten-foot ceiling. It was furnished more like an apartment in New York than Corinth, which was not a coincidence. She had seen a movie that had an apartment setting that she fell in love with. When the movie came out on videotape, she bought it and studied every detail of the setting before buying furniture. In the end, she replicated the set in the movie. She, of course, was the only one who knew this small piece of personal information. When the door bell rang, she flipped a black switch on an intercom by her front door and learned that the private detective from Jackson was downstairs and wanted to talk with her. She invited him to come upstairs to apartment number two, feeling fortunate that she had already showered and dressed. She opened the door and invited him in.

"Care for some hot tea?" she asked with a smile.

"Thank you," he replied.

She sat him down at a table in a large living/dining area and she disappeared into the kitchen, returning in a few minutes with two cups, two tea bags and a pot of boiling water. She poured the water almost ritually into the cups and placed the tea bags in the hot liquid. They chatted about good nutrition and hot weather and Lake Pickwick until she finally smiled and said, "Okay, tell me what you want to know. You didn't come here to talk about the weather."

"No," he said. "I wanted to talk about banana pudding."

"Ha!" she laughed out loud. "I see that you discovered Miss Melanie's little obsession."

"Was it really that bad?"

"Oh, it was worse. She was an addict to it like a junkie to heroin. It was serious. Of course, everybody made it worse by taking banana pudding to her all the time. She was sick, I tell you."

"Your brother couldn't do anything about it?"

"He tried," she said. "He was on the verge of sending her to a treatment facility. She really was making his life miserable, not to mention the danger to her own health."

"What did she think about the idea?"

"She resisted, I'm sure."

"Did your brother ever talk to you about this problem with his wife?"

"Yes," she said, pausing to sip her last drop of tea. "We had what you might call a family meeting about it." She took a deep breath and exhaled. Her eyes began to water, but no tears fell. "Marlin told us that he appreciated everything we did for him, but that he had made a choice when he married Melanie. He even said that it may have been the wrong choice. He told us that she had an eating problem and migraines, but that they were going to work through it. He was very worried about her because of the headaches and her taking so much pain medicine. He told us he needed our support. We all cried and held hands and said sort of a prayer. It was a very emotional time for all of us."

"Did he specifically mention acetaminophen?"

"Yes," she said. "Marlin told us that too much at one time after taking so much on a regular basis could be fatal. He told her that too."

"When was this meeting?"

"Early June, I guess. Maybe the second week in June."

"Where was it held?"

"At Sally's house."

"What time of day?"

"Morning," she replied. "Maybe I should say office hours. He couldn't meet with us any other time. Melanie wouldn't let him see anybody except his patients at the office."

"She really sounds insecure," commented Boulder.

"It was bad. Marlin's health was beginning to deteriorate, too. We worried about him."

Boulder took a sip of tea and looked around the large living room. In one corner was a computer station and small desk. "I see you are into the electronic age. Are you connected to the Internet?"

"Yes, of course."

"Do you mind if I check my e-mail? I haven't had a chance to do that since I've been in Corinth."

She stood up and walked over to the computer. She

made a few keystrokes and then offered him the chair.

"I am connected to my Internet Service Provider. Is that all you need?"

"Yes," said Boulder. "I can go to mine and check my mail from here."

"Be my guest," she said. "I'm going to dry my hair."

He sat down and she left the room. He heard the hair dryer in the bathroom. He pulled up her "old mail" file and looked for one from Sally. He found it quickly and opened it. He looked toward the bathroom, making sure she was still drying her hair. He clicked on the icon to print and waited while the printer hummed and a green light came on. He could hear the familiar sound of the printer about to laser print onto paper. As the paper flowed through the printer he heard the hair dryer stop. He took a deep breath and clicked on an icon that would close the file. It would not respond while printing. He glanced back toward the bathroom, alert to her walking in the room. There was a final click on the printer and he yanked the paper out, folded it and put it in his pants pocket. His heart was racing.

It was five more minutes before she returned. He checked his e-mail and found that two new clients wanted him to call about cases. There was a ton of the usual junk mail. When she walked in he was signing off the account.

"Get any mail?" she said cheerily.

"Just the usual," he said.

They continued talking for 30 more minutes. The subject of Pace McHatten came up and she said that he had not been the same since Melanie came into Marlin's life. Marlin and Pace had been lifelong friends. They even owned a cabin together on Pickwick Lake.

The detective left and went back to his room at the Generals' Quarters. He took out the piece of paper from his pocket and studied it.

Subj:The Recipe
Date:July 21
From: SHaines1145d@sixroads.net (Sally Haines)
To:Sylvia1922@corinthnet.com.

Syl—here's the banana pudding recipe. Don't forget the most important ingredient.

1 vanilla instant pudding
2 c. milk
1 can sweetened condensed milk
1 package whipped topping
vanilla wafers
bananas
D. Angel mushrooms

Mix pudding, dried mushrooms and milk until thick. Add condensed milk and whipped topping. Layer bananas, cookies and pudding mixture.

Something wasn't quite right. What was it?

Boulder went back to the Generals' Quarters. As he walked in, Ann Beckwith approached and said, "You have a message to call Laura in Jackson. She said it was urgent."

Boulder thanked her, went up to his room and called Laura's office.

"Jack, I came in this morning and did some research on poisonings, like I said I would." She was almost breathless.

"Yes?"

"I found a case where a woman was poisoned with acetaminophen and it was appealed to the State Supreme Court on several issues," she said. "It's very similar to your case."

"Good," said Boulder.

"I'm afraid it's not so good, Jack," she said. "It was a case out of Tupelo and the defense attorney was none other than Pace McHatten, Sr."

"I think it's time to call the district attorney."

Chapter 15

It was 10:00 a.m. on Thursday. At the request of District Attorney William Magowan, a meeting had been called to discuss the case of the death of Melanie Haines. It was agreed that it would be held at the law offices of Pace McHatten. Assembled in the large conference room of the law firm were the following persons:

William Magowan, District Attorney

Magnolia Young, Assistant District Attorney

Pace McHatten, Sr., Attorney for Dr. Marlin Haines

Marlin Haines, M.D.

Sylvia Haines McChester

Sadie Haines Kellog

Sally Haines

Jack Boulder

The district attorney called the meeting to order. "Yesterday, Mr. Boulder here came to my office and shared the results of his investigation into the death of Melanie Haines. Some of what he says is fact and some is speculation. Based on my investigation, we feel that this matter should go to the grand jury right away since the evidence is rather conclusive. Nevertheless, to help clear up this investigation I have asked Mr. Boulder to share with all of you what he did with me. As an elected official I want to make sure that I am fair to all parties. It's all yours, Mr. Boulder."

"As you all know, I have spent the last few days in Corinth investigating the death of Melanie Haines, wife of Dr. Marlin Haines. It might be more appropriate to say that I was hired to prove that Dr. Haines didn't kill his wife. Since it's hard to prove a negative, I figured I had to find out who did it. I think I have been successful in my mission."

He paused to let his comments sink in, figuring everybody would look around wondering who was the murderer in their midst. He was wrong. Nobody moved.

"Allow me to go down the list of suspects. First and foremost is Dr. Haines himself," he said looking at what had become a tired old man. "Dr. Haines is a good suspect, since he has motive and opportunity. The problem with him as a suspect is credibility. Does anybody really believe that a doctor would poison his wife in his own home and discover the body himself? It's just too convenient. So let's come back to him.

"Next, we have the Haines sisters. Loyal and devoted to their brother. A conspiracy among them to kill their brother's wife would make sense. There are several ways they could have done it. First, they could have done it together. Second, they could have done it individually. They might have even done it in some combination. In the beginning I really thought they were the ones who had done it. They too had motive and even opportunity. The possibilities are intriguing.

Each could have had a small share in it that individually would not have been enough to kill Melanie, but together could have added up. For example, three bowls of pudding each laced with acetaminophen would have done the trick. The district attorney here would have had a heck of a time proving that one. And quite frankly, I have no doubt they are capable of such.

"There was a conspiracy among them. They tried to distract me with a trail of poison mushrooms. That was ingenious." He looked at Sally. "Leaving an e-mail in your computer addressed to Sylvia just for me to see. I especially liked the e-mail signal going off while I was at your house. Did you pre-arrange that with Sylvia? To send a message while I was there?" Sally inhaled and crossed her arms. A tinge of red blushed her face. "Fortunately I was able to see that message again on Sylvia's computer." He reached in his pocket and pulled out a piece of paper. "And here it is." He tossed it on the table and it was immediately picked up by the district attorney. "Take a look at the date."

"July twenty-first," said Magowan, with a puzzled look.

"Exactly," said Boulder. "Melanie died on June 18. That e-mail message was created over a month later. As a matter of fact, it was created the day I interviewed the Haines sisters. My guess is that Sylvia and Sadie called Sally after we met at Martha's Menu. Is that how it happened, Sally?"

"You tell us, Mr. Private Detective!" said Sally Haines, her teeth clenched.

"You planted an interesting diversion—pun intended," said Boulder. "Poison mushrooms. Very creative. The reason you did that was to create doubt and remove suspicion from Marlin. I admit that you had me going for awhile."

"Now let's turn to a new suspect," said Boulder. He turned and said, "Pace McHatten."

McHatten's thick eyebrows went up like those on a judge who had heard an attorney use an obscene word in his court. "I beg your pardon."

"Marlin was your lifelong friend, wasn't he?" challenged Boulder.

"Yes."

"You two spent a lot of time together, and even owned a cabin together, didn't you?"

"So what?" demanded McHatten.

"Melanie took away your best friend, didn't she?"

"Get to the point," said McHatten.

"You were jealous of her, weren't you?"

Magowan leaned his head forward ever so slightly and narrowed his eyebrows. His eyes focused directly on McHatten. All other eyes turned toward the senior lawyer. Only Dr. Haines stared straight ahead, seemingly oblivious to the conversation going on around him.

"You also knew about her condition, and that too

much acetaminophen could be fatal. Dr. Haines told you that, didn't he?"

"What is this? We deal in evidence in this business. Get to it," said McHatten.

"I will do just that," said Boulder. "I think I just established that you had motive. Now, let's deal with opportunity. On Thursday, June seventeenth, the day before Melanie Haines died of acetaminophen toxicity, you had your secretary purchase three large bottles of acetaminophen capsules at the drug store on the square. She brought them back to you in this room, and you placed them in the bottom right hand drawer of your desk. The next morning you had her deliver a large bowl of banana pudding to Melanie Haines, didn't you?"

"What?" McHatten bellowed indignantly. "How dare you!"

Dr. Haines turned his head and looked without expression at his best friend. There was a long silence.

"It could have been a suicide," said Dr. Haines softly.

"Yes, Doctor, it could have been," said Boulder. "It also could have been you. Or it could have been one of two other people in this room."

They began looking around at each other. Magowan was getting impatient. "Hurry up, Mr. Boulder," he said.

"Yes, sir," said Boulder. "All we need to eliminate

Mr. McHatten here is to look in the bottom right hand drawer of his desk."

Boulder could not have called more attention to a piece of furniture if he had said that there was a bomb inside it. Everyone turned toward the desk. Boulder walked across the room and stood behind the massive desk. For some reason, he became aware of its power. He felt strong with it in front of him, giving him authority as he surveyed the subjects beyond him in the large room. He reached down, opened the drawer and removed a bag that contained three large bottles of pain reliever. He reached in the bag and found a receipt from Borroum's Drug Store. The piece of paper was dated June 17. He walked back to the conference table and placed the contents of the bag on the tabletop.

"What were you going to do with so much medicine?" asked Boulder rhetorically. He did not expect an answer. "It's probably best that we never know."

"You said there was another suspect," said District Attorney Magowan. "Who might that be?"

"Yes, that leaves us with one more suspect," said Boulder. "One who also had motive and opportunity." He took a deep breath and said, "Sadie, would you like to tell us what was in the bowl you delivered on the morning of June eighteenth? There was more than banana pudding in it, wasn't there?"

Sadie Haines McChester began crying. Softly at first. Then sobbing. Not knowing how to react, they all just sat there like an elementary school class after some-one has just had an accident in his pants.

"Let's come to order," said Pace McHatten, like the judge he used to be. Then turning toward the sobbing sister of his old friend, he said, "It's alright, Sadie."

"It was an accident," Sadie sobbed. "An awful acci-dent. Please believe me."

"Why don't you tell us what happened?" said Boulder sympathetically.

"I . . . I didn't mean to . . ." she stammered.

"Just a moment," said Pace McHatten, taking con-trol. "As Ms. McChester's attorney I am advising her not to say anything else. And unless anybody has any-thing further, this meeting is adjourned."

There was a hush in the room for a moment. Then everyone stood up, just like in court, and slowly left the room. Sally and Sylvia wanted to stay, but McHatten shooed them out. All that remained were McHatten, Boulder and Sadie. McHatten placed a box of tissues in front of her, and she buried her face in the soft, white paper. McHatten and Boulder just stood in place, look-ing down at the floor while she got it out. Finally, she spoke.

Looking up at McHatten, she said, "She was just supposed to get a little sicker. She wasn't supposed to die. If she got a little sicker, Marlin was going to take her to Memphis to a place where she could live for awhile."

"It will be alright, Sadie," said McHatten.

"Am I going to jail?"

"No," he said reassuringly. "You did not intention-ally commit a crime. And I will be your lawyer if you need one."

"Thank you, Pace," she said hopefully. "You've always been there when the Haines needed you."

She got up and went to the arms of Pace McHatten. He held her and comforted her as Jack Boulder walked out the door unnoticed.

Downstairs, District Attorney Magowan told his assistant to move on to more serious cases. This one did not need to be pursued anymore.

Chapter 16

There are thousands of soldiers buried in and around Corinth, Mississippi. Monument-sized headstones and small markers identify the resting places. In every grave rests someone who was loved by someone else. The memory of the wars, conflicts and campaigns in which the soldiers died lives on, preserved by historians and interested others. The memory of the individuals, however, is often lost when their loved ones pass on, and only the headstones and markers remain. Of all the graves of Corinth, only one had any interest to Jack Boulder. It was the one that contained the remains of Pace McHatten, Jr., the Army buddy who died in his arms in Vietnam.

Boulder had checked out of the Generals' Quarters just after noon, vowing that he would come back and show Laura the beauty and hospitality of the home. A summer thunderstorm had developed over a three-square mile section of town and dropped buckets of rain in its path. The storm had passed and the last of the rain water was flowing in the gutters that surrounded the cemetery where Pace McHatten, Jr. was buried. Boulder stood on the wet ground staring at the head-stone. It had Pace's name, his date of birth and death. There was no indication that he had ever served in the military. Boulder understood Pace much better now, why he wanted to get away from his father and why he kept things inside himself. Pace McHatten, Sr. was not a man whom a boy would want to show off as a father. Boulder closed his eyes and attempted to say a proper prayer, but neither words nor thoughts would come.

"You loved him, didn't you?" It was the voice of Pace McHatten behind. Boulder did not turn around.

"Yes," he said, still facing the grave.

"And you hate me, don't you."

"I hate what you did to him," said Boulder.

"Would you mind turning around?" asked McHatten.

"I'm fine," said Boulder, not moving.

There was a squishing sound on the wet ground as McHatten walked alongside Boulder, then stood in front of him beside the headstone. "I want to show you something that I never showed my son." He reached in the pocket of the same seersucker suit and held out a medal on the end of a dark blue cloth necklace trimmed in red and white. The medal was gold, and contained an eagle with wings spread on a cross. Boulder recognized it immediately as the country's second highest military decoration. It was given for exceptional heroism in combat.

"That's a Distinguished Service Cross. What . . . ? What are you doing with that?"

"It might help explain some of the things I've done."

"Is that yours?" asked Boulder. "Pace never told me you had the DSC."

"Pace didn't know I was awarded this medal."

116

"What did you do to get it?"

"I was on Normandy Beach on D-Day. It was hell on earth. No one should have to go through that." He reached down and unbuttoned his shirt to reveal an ugly scar on the side of his rib cage. "Shrapnel. It still hurts when I cough. I hate winter. Can't stand to get a cold." He closed his shirt and continued. "I went into World War II full of you-know-what and vigor, just like you and Pace did in Vietnam. But one day, when I stuck a bayonet in the neck of a German boy and saw the blood spurt from his artery I decided I couldn't take it anymore. Oh, I did my duty and served my hitch. When I got home I used to go out to the Shiloh Battlefield and think about war and what it accomplished. Which is nothing, by the way. I vowed my son would never go to war. Wouldn't even let him take ROTC. I told him that I would forbid his enlisting in the military and would disown him if he did. Well, he did and I did. Now, he's dead from combat and I'm a miserable old man who let war stand between a father and a son."

"Did you ever tell him about your service?" asked Boulder.

"No," he said sadly. "I took great pains to hide it from him. I was afraid that if I glorified the military he would want to enlist even more. I guess I went overboard with it."

"I think I understand."

"I'll never be able to make it up to him," he said,

nodding towards Pace's grave. "But for some reason, I want you to have this. You were his closest friend. He used to write about you in his letters. Looking back, I should have told him instead of trying to protect him so much. I just didn't want him to go through what I went through."

"I can understand that," said Boulder. "It's only natural."

His bottom lip began quivering. "I wish I could hear Pace say that."

"Judge McHatten, I'm not Pace, but he and I were like brothers. I'm sure he would say the same thing."

"I apologize to you, too. I didn't treat you very well while you were in Corinth. That's not like us here. I hope you will come back and let me show you a little more hospitality."

"That would be nice," said Boulder. "I'll have to miss that Slugburger thing this year. Maybe next time."

"The Slugburger Festival—an event that should not be missed. But that's a year away. There are plenty of things between now and then. Don't wait that long."

"I won't," said Boulder.

McHatten handed him the medal with his left hand, and shook hands with his right hand. Boulder walked back to his car and drove away. Pace McHatten, Sr. turned around to his son's grave and said softly, "Thank you for forgiving me, son."